MAGICAL
ELK

MAGICAL ELK

A NOVELLA

JASON DURANT

Book design by Maureen Cutajar
www.gopublished.com

ISBN: 978-1-7334407-5-2

ALSO BY JASON DURANT

Kiss da Wolf: A Novel
A Wound in the Earth: A Novel
Witherpools: A Story Collection
The Crowd of Distant Echoes: A Novel

Contents

MAGICAL ELK

THE RIBS OF MAN

One

⧗ THE CABIN ⧗

It is night, a white moon all but hidden. Footfalls sound through the mountains as summer smoke drifts overhead. Jim Lasher sits in his cabin in the fragrant brush and tinder far from his Los Angeles home preparing for bloody, ritualistic war with nonhuman beings. The footfalls crash, build, and then fade into a silent runic dimension of symbols and incantations, where they become a thing rhythmically imposed. Creative confusion visits Jim often and he fears they are reshaping him somehow.

Nothing is sacred anymore. Nothing is ordinary anymore. Everything occurs within a smashed or demented context. Mental landscapes are absurd beyond recognition, so Jim writes everything down. Later, he retrieves what he's written and glues it all back together. It's how he maintains continuity with himself. With his world. It's how he defies the invaders.

The invaders come slashing down to earth night after night, brilliant flashes and streamers of light, like a fireworks display or aurora borealis, only more so. It is military in nature: clusters, groups, arrays, and lone individuals shooting down.

Jim knows that not many people can see these lights. He has always been blessed with a special gift of seeing. He often counsels people, even total strangers, and somehow knows just exactly what to say to trigger a big change in their lives.

He doesn't know if the government is aware of this invading force, if he should warn them, if others with this gift have approached them. He wants to start doing something. Gather people. Pray. Or maybe not pray. Hell. He doesn't know. Tell them to go back to their birthplaces. Tell them to be with their families.

Despite his gift of seeing, Jim has not discerned the end game of the invaders. He thinks it can't be good. He feels they enter people's lives at subtle levels and run deadly, manipulative games. What madness it is.

As a lookout in this war, Jim believes he has discovered the light beings' schemata: They take shape as familiars; they are transcendent; they are doctrinaire, mesmerizing you and serving you as God before wiping you out.

You do not want to meet a light being carelessly. You strengthen yourself first. You become more powerful or you go up in smoke. Jim threads himself through the changes now, his pen smoldering across the paper. He dreads seeing the first one tonight. He feels it will be his older son, Spencer, knocking on the door. He'd rather it be his younger son, Rory. In any case, nothing will ever be the same.

A few nights ago, Jim woke from a dream in which he saw himself putting two smooth rocks on either side of the footpath leading up to his cabin. He sensed it was an instruction from the light beings. He felt it would create an entrance. A doorway. An invitation. He wrestled with himself, but went out and set two smooth rocks in place, like in the dream. They gleamed in the darkness. He has felt the presence of other instructions. Deeper instructions. He will not dwell on that. His life would be over. He will write things down. He will acquire power.

Jim hears a knock at the door. A soldier appears in his mind. Spencer left the University of Virginia four years ago and enlisted in the Army. Rory informs him that Spencer has become an Army Special Forces officer.

Jim continues to write. He wants the visitor to be Spencer but not Spencer. Does that make sense? Is that possible? Why shape it this way? He knows. It's fear.

Jim won't answer the knock until he's got it shaped; he wants answers from whoever is there. It's a customary request and hasn't bit him yet. He wants to learn from this visitor.

Do not have Spencer kill me, he writes. *Have Spencer give me knowledge of the invaders.*

He sets his journal aside. He has dozens of journals lying around, works in progress. He rises from his chair and walks to the door.

He wishes the dog were with him. The dog went missing a day ago. His daughter, Katrina, was going to come up to the cabin and pick up the dog and take it home. Too late. Too bad. It was a good dog. A golden retriever. A big dog. But gentle as a baby.

He called Katrina and told her the dog was missing and not to come up to the cabin and get it. Katrina wanted to come anyway. Her mom, Renée, would drive her. She said she'd walk through the woods looking for it. No, Jim had said. Don't come. Katrina did not like to hear him say that. She didn't weep, though. Before calling, he'd written: *Do not let Katrina weep when I tell her about the dog.* He hates to hear her weep.

Katrina is sixteen and in many ways a baby. She lives in L.A. with Renée, Jim's estranged wife. Jim plans to write Renée back into his life. When first married, they'd both wanted to go to Venice, Italy, but never did. He'll ask her to go now. It might not be their birthplace, but it is a link. They'll take Katrina. Spencer and Rory are from Jim's earlier marriage, to a woman who died young. He feels Renée will say yes.

He grasps the doorknob and feels a presence.

Jim sometimes dreams of being an apprentice angel while still in flesh, training for when he will be in spirit. He has spent his whole life helping others, now he's afraid and wonders: Who will help me? He feels someone will. We are all pieces of one soul. He will write that thought down later.

He opens the door.

It's a California Highway Patrol Officer.

He is a big man and wears a big hat and has a big gun on his belt. His face flickers red and orange in the flames from the interior cabin lights. He looks serious.

"Evening," the cop says. "Glad I found you here."

"Evening," Jim says.

"Stay inside tonight," the cop says. "Someone's missing. Pets have gone missing, too. We think there's a mountain lion about."

"Oh my god! My dog is missing! Can you take a report?"

"I can."

"Please come inside."

Jim steps aside and watches the officer charge in, a tall man with boots that click and a wide-brimmed hat that soars above all else and eyes that sweep up everything.

"Nice rustic cabin you have here, Mr. Lasher. I like the feel of this place."

"Yes, I like the feel of it, too."

The cop takes his hat off and sets it on the table and then takes a notebook out of his shirt pocket and he and Jim pull out chairs and take seats, the chairs scraping across the wooden floor. They are in the kitchen, which is contiguous with the living room and entryway.

They settle their weight upon the chairs.

"Nice cobblestone walk outside," the cop says. "I couldn't see it too well, but I could feel it underfoot."

"Yes," Jim says. "I put it in myself. I did a lot of the work up here over the years. It's good therapy. Work of any sort is good therapy."

"If you say, but I think work will squeeze the piss out of you quicker than anything else. In any case, it's necessary for survival."

"It is that, too."

"What kind of dog did you have?"

Jim tells the cop all he knows about the dog. The cop writes his report in a busy, energetic fashion with such intensity it shakes the table.

Done with his report on the dog, the cop sets his notebook aside. And now the cop's voice acquires claws that dig in.

"Show ID and answer all questions," the officer says.

Jim shows him his California driver's license and while doing so takes a closer look at him. The cop is not a young man. The terrain of his face is deeply etched and his flesh sags from too much living. He has a large head, fair skin, and eyes that drift like wayward smoke. But the cop is not all sloppy. Jim sees the toughness in the cast of his shoulders and in the massive architecture of his hands.

The cop gives him back his driver's license. "You look like a ghost, Mr. Lasher, all wispy and blown away. Someone needs to dip your nerves in ice water."

"Please—"

"We are one and the same, Mr. Lasher. Different aspects, I believe."

"Please, call me Jim."

"All right, Jim. And you can call me Horse."

"Horse? Is that really your name?"

"I'd rather not say."

"Well, Horse, I guess the difference between you and me is one of degree," Jim says.

"I guess it is."

Horse seems to have entered a somnambulant haze, his manner and speech strange and erratic. In an unguarded moment of black-and-white clarity, Jim thinks he sees Horse flash a knife toward him and slash his right carotid artery and bleed him out.

"Fuck you, Horse!"

It was an unconscious motor reflex.

Horse lunges across the table with the knife and plunges it in but Jim lurches back and the knife misses his carotid artery and tears through his shirt and sticks flesh about six inches above Jim's belt.

Jim yelps, his motor reflexes propelling him backward. He crashes to the floor and screeches out words in an injured, angry, made-up language.

Horse is on his feet. Jim rotates his body toward him and assumes a ferocious posture, holding up his chair, waving it, teetering between leaping off the floor at Horse in a rage and leaping from the cabin in terror.

"I'm hurt! Damn you! You stuck me with that knife!"

Looking down at his torso where blood is soaking into his shirt, he emits a howl like that of a dog caught in the jaws of a coyote. In ritual fashion, he spreads his shirt flat against his side, trying to stem the flow of blood.

Horse comes around the table, leans close, brings Jim's head up with a fistful of hair, and puts the tip of his knife against the flesh under Jim's right eye.

Jim releases the chair, clamps his hands on Horse's wrist, tries to shove his arm away, but can't budge it.

Jim composes something in his mind, an act of shaping. He won't let Spencer kill him. It is Spencer. It has to be.

Let Spencer and me go on the road. On a trip. Let the trip be meaningful for us. Let Spencer hurt me, if he must, but don't let him kill me.

And instantly Jim is sorry for what he did. He thinks he shaped it wrong. He thinks it will mean big trouble for him.

Horse's voice explodes.

"Get us back on the road you motherfucking whore or I'll do more than stick you—I'll cut your fucking heart out."

In utter slow motion, Jim removes his hands from Horse's wrist. For a moment, his hands seem to leave the normal order of things and become winds with no predictability. Horse keeps the tip of his knife buried in the fleshy spot beneath Jim's eye, and Jim's hands soon sag.

"Put it in gear," Horse says. "Steer the motherfucker and keep your eyes on the road."

"I'm not driving anything."

"Well then you'd better get started."

"Damn you!"

"Speed up! Go! Go! Go!"

"Damn you!"

"Get up to highway speed, motherfucker."

"You're the motherfucker."

Horse pulls his knife away from Jim's eye and sticks him in the ribs, drawing a second blood trail onto his shirt. Jim hunches, makes sounds in his made-up language, like a choir of wounded animals howling out their anguish. He turns his head toward Horse, his eyes struggling, his voice hollow and wet.

"I still can't believe it. If you got my lung, I'm dead."

"I didn't get your lung. If I wanted your lung, I'd have had it. Easy-peasy."

"Motherfucker!"

"You aren't dead yet, so move it."

"Horse, I'm hurt."

"Yeah? Well, you asked for it." The cop backs away and heads for the door.

"No, wait."

"It's always wait," the cop says. "Nothing ever happens. No dreams come true."

"They do."

"Never. Nothing works."

"Why didn't you give school a try? That could have been your magical elk."

"I did. They destroyed me."

"They didn't destroy you."

"They did. They're not like me. How would you know?"

"I went to school. They didn't destroy me."

"They did, Jim. They keep you in a box. You don't know it."

Horse walks back to him.

"Careful with that knife," Jim says. "Why don't you become an expert with the knife? And teach knife skills? That could be your magical elk."

"The one who holds the knife is always the expert. Now get me my magical elk."

"You'll get it. But what about the next one? Won't you need another magical elk soon?"

"Not if this one's big enough."

"Horse, this is crazy. You don't need to do this."

"I need to. I've got the knife. I'll plunge it in."

"What other place?"

"Huh?"

"Horse, you just said you needed to do this to get to that other place."

"No, I didn't."

"You did. What is this other place?"

"Jim, it's the place where things get done fast and weird."

"You're insane."

"No. Saner than ever. I see things differently when I stick someone."

"When have you killed?"

"Stick doesn't always mean kill, though it can. I killed in the Army. In Nam."

"Nam was long ago. You aren't old enough for Nam."

"No. It's now. Today."

"You're crazy."

"I'm sane. When I stick someone, I see something on the other side of Vinita."

"Vinita? You know her?"

"We all know a little about Vinita, okay? We all know. I see something on the other side of her."

"What do you see?"

"Us. You. Me. Others. They're hanging us out to dry. It's why I've got the knife. I see soldiers, though I don't think they're real. Not like we know real."

"You're nuts. What does the philosopher Horse think of all this?"

"I'm not always the philosopher. That's why I've got the knife."

"Well, can you elucidate?"

"Yeah. When I'm stuck or spread to somewhere, then it comes to me."

"The knife comes to you?"

"Philosophy comes to me. I'll elucidate further. How'd you become a doctor?"

"I'm not a doctor."

"A PhD, then."

"I studied."

"No, really, how?"

"I went to school."

"Something made it certain you would become a doctor."

"That sounds religious."

"No. The universe is antireligious. Religious people invent meaning that vaporizes as the universe reveals more of itself. The last revelation from Vinita was, 'We are dead, but don't know it.' If that's true, religion is a corpse."

"I guess. How'd you know what she said?"

"Vinita is boundless, more than the mind can hold all at once. She is suspected of being entirety, and we cannot know her without knowing all. We see her when our vision loops, then Vinita takes shape. Also, I've got the knife."

"I know. You'll stick me in the ribs."

"Drive safe. Popping pills?"

"Pills?"

"Everything's a pill. But none of them work unless you think they will. I have the knife."

"In my ribs."

"The knife's a pill."

"Yeah, I know. I believe it."

"Get me my magical elk, Jim. You never even ask me what my magical elk is."

"Okay, what's your magical elk?"

"A vision."

"You see a vision?"

"Yes, over and over. There is some kind of trouble as the universe reveals the next big step. Religious people are tired; they need to dry up. Changes coming. Big changes. See?"

"You'll get your money. That's your magical elk."

"No. You lied. It's okay. I'll get my magical elk."

"Money?"

"No, I want to see what they do to us in that other place beyond Vinita. It's a vision I get when I'm on the edge."

"I'm on the edge. I don't see any vision."

"You might not. I do. I'm a philosopher. The universe gave me that. I think that's why I see the vision. You see pills."

"I see pills?"

"Yeah. The universe gave you pills."

"Horse, do I have a magical elk?"

"You have pills."

"Do they help?"

"Look in the mirror, Jim. What do you think?"

"What about your vision? Does that help?"

"Yes. In my vision I think about philosophy. It's a death vision. When we're vanquished, I see it."

"Again and again?"

"Yes. It never ends. They hang us up."

"And the religious people are dead?"

"They died out. Long ago. Now just ghosts. No substance. Just rhetoric. Worthless. What counts is something real. Stories are real. They are the doorways."

"You get this vision. And I get pills?"

"Yes."

"And others?"

"They get one thing or the other. Vision or pills. Something's happening to tear the cataracts off. Now we see. That's what I think. To get your magical elk, first rule: make the philosophers mad, then you have a chance to learn."

"That's the magical elk? Make the philosophers mad?"

"Yes. The philosophers. Or the teachers. Make them mad. Religion is mad. We're getting a chance, Jim. Don't blow it."

Jim's left side has been killing him since before the border crossing, folding up on him, and again he feels shame for having drawn this makeshift condition from a dishonorable universe and for always being in search of an escape.

With one swipe of the knife, Horse slices through Jim's lips.

Making ghastly sounds that fill the cabin, Jim whips out a large white handkerchief and presses it against his lips, the white material drawing bright red blossoms of blood. Holding the handkerchief in place, his eyes become diamond-hard squiggles that stare at Horse.

"Do you feel better, Horse, giving me more of your pain?"

"I think there is no hunting partner. I think you made it up."

"I didn't make it up!" Jim's words explode through his bloody lips and handkerchief.

"So where is this farm of Vinita's?"

"Up ahead."

"Where?"

"Ahead."

"I think you wear a mask so big it obscures your whole face."

"You're wrong!" Another explosion from Jim. With this one, he hits Horse with a spray of blood.

Two

⊠ THE FARMHOUSE ⊠

Jim is on the highway with Horse, a crack in the east fast arising. He takes an exit, drives a few miles, then turns onto a gravel road. They head into the sun. It blazes a circle around them, turning everything into a yellow fury. Jim turns in at a wooded farmstead and drives along a pitched, rutted road.

Through a stand of sunlit cottonwood and spruce, Jim sees the farmhouse and shudders. For one terrifying instant, the farmhouse had morphed into the monstrous demon Baphomet, a goat-headed figure that symbolizes duality. A shrill alarm goes off inside him. Something is not right. Some dark, bygone era seems to be present, weighing the atmosphere down with something oppressive.

He shakes his head and looks around. The place looks derelict. This isn't Vinita's place.

He pulls up near the house, stops the Jeep, turns the engine off. He leaps from the Jeep and runs. He has something in his hand, concealing it.

Horse springs out and gives chase.

Jim's feet carry him along, a single drop of blood rolling down the hand that holds the handkerchief to his sliced lips, the puncture wounds under his ribs deep pools of worsening effects.

Jim dashes around the corner of an outbuilding, inhaling the flower-garden scents that flow through the yard, Horse closing fast on him.

He tears toward a stand of trees, beyond which lies a vast field of wheat ablaze in the rising sun. He'll have to kill Horse. He's a big dog that bites.

He whirls around, looks for him, sees him. He aims a handgun at him, fires off several rounds, pauses, fires again and runs. He pulled the gun from Horse's belt when Horse was eyeing the farmhouse.

In the wheat field, Jim stops and fires at Horse again.

Click.

Horse lengthens his stride, leaps upon Jim, takes him down, slaps the empty gun away, rolls him over, finds placement for his knife. From a spot under the ribs, he drives the knife upward into Jim's chest, just as Jim's left hand whips out in a disciplined move and whacks Horse hard on the side of the neck.

⧗

A sudden surge in blood pressure shocks Horse's brain and he goes limp. Feeling faraway electrical tingles, he tries to get to his feet but is too wobbly to make it. His eyes become big, sloppy animals that watch Jim pull the knife out of his chest and turn it around.

Horse, limp, falls on the blade.

Horse rolls on the ground, eases to his feet, and stumbles away, holding on to the knife imbedded in his chest. His fingers are a blood-soaked mess. His mind is arcing into madness. How had Jim done that? How? Jim was dead—not yet, but soon. Jim made Horse limp, got the knife out, turned it around.

Did you ever consider medicine?

Jim is a metaphysician of sorts and knows dark, lethal secrets.

Horse collapses, lies on the ground a good distance from Jim. He forces his head up, sees a lump of Jim on the ground, no movement, bleeding out.

Horse's consciousness begins poking through the chaos of all that has happened to him, and soon sharp pains like sun-blackened beetles crawl over him, alighting into the jagged recesses of his chest.

He tries to shut out the misery. Horse needs to be clear. He has to assess the cause. Jim has a staring eye. It stared at the wrong person. It stared at Vinita Scoggins and that's what led to all of this. But he knows that isn't true. The real cause always lies beyond the observable mess.

He thinks of Vinita—the last time he stood close to her, touched her, positioned her; her brunette hair unique, long and thick with undulating curls; pulling it back, her ears and neck naked. He inhales her perfume, her fear, her growing excitement—and the universe opens up for Horse, and he is swept away to a place where he is given an animal name. They are forcing him to abandon the old ways.

A commando called Tarantula tells him the exercise is designed to pull him deeper into their realm.

They tell him to relax and walk around.

"What's this thing in my brain?" Horse asks.

"It's in everyone's brain," Tarantula says. "Your brain constantly paints a picture for you and colors that picture with sights, sounds, smells, and tastes. But when something new enters—something monstrous—the brain rejects the new information because it would complicate, confuse, and distort the recipient's world too much."

"But it doesn't fit."

"New information that doesn't fit will nevertheless be forced to fit, but with much falsifying by the brain, an organ that likes consistency, harmony, and coherence. Your brain will lie to you."

"But why do I feel this murderous heat rising?"

"Your brain is preparing a nice, neat, orderly path for you to kill. A cozy path. You will feel totally justified."

Horse walks around in the field of wheat, his hands clutching the knife in his chest, blood soaking his fingers, as the commandos continue to circle him and stare into his eyes.

Horse falls to earth, like the moon smacking soft against it, getting its white, round face dirty. In a half-flicker of awareness, he senses a massive, powerful, camouflaged organ of control behind the visible clutter. And then his awareness becomes like that of an animal stirring and poking its head up—a prism through which he absorbs sharp edges, soft roundness, and quick movement, but nothing of a higher order.

Through this prism he sees soldiers in black hoods jog onto the field carrying two stout poles about ten feet long and a posthole digger. In minutes, the soldiers have the bodies of Horse and Jim hanging upright on the poles, feet dangling.

⧗

Mirror time. The bedroom on the upper floor of the farmhouse is lit by a spray of sunlight through the window. Through this dimness, Jim Lasher moves like a shadow, carrying the hand basin which he'd filled with water downstairs. Once again he has to reposition the weighty dresser mirror to catch the precious drops of sun. His heavy torso hangs in front of him, grizzled hair matting his chest, his shoulders hunched, favoring his three distinct thoracic wounds. His sliced-open lips in their swelling and bloodiness resemble things chewed by noxious elves.

He sets the hand basin on the dresser, dips cupped hands into the water, and draws them to his lips. He's already flushed his wounds dozens of times, not daring to stop, fearing nature's killing bureaucracy: deadly infection. The very thought of dying in this most officious manner brings liveliness to his mind and body and sets his focus laser sharp. He will give his lips a final cleansing, avoid this attempt by nature to do him in, and win the battle.

The hand basin runs red as he draws handful after handful of water to his lips. When he sees that his lip wounds have attained a scowling, pink puffiness, he leaves them alone. Leaving wounds open allows them to drain, and is the best way to guard against infection. Later, he'll suture the lip wounds closed, though he'll leave the puncture wounds in his torso open.

Window time. He is a pair of eyes staring out the upper-floor bedroom window of the farmhouse, the sun drizzling on the field of wheat, recovering as if from sickness or a strong kick to the head. He backs away from the window, his torso still bare. He'd applied Mercurochrome to his thoracic wounds and that might have been a mistake. He is still blinking the sting away. He should have diluted the Mercurochrome first. He goes back to the window. Blink and blink again.

The whole experience is still raw in his brain, the molecules still lining up, an aura of death pervading him.

Jim lives for knowledge, to create value, to move the human race forward, but lately he feels a stranger to all that is good.

He'd been seeing Vinita Scoggins in Montana. Vinita was not imagination, but real. The guy beside him in the Jeep was a different matter. That guy's reality remains a question.

Jim pops a pill, a puff of muzzle smoke for his brain, and walks to the dresser and looks in the mirror. Damn it. He cut me. Twice. Three times. Stings. He shudders. His lips are the worst. Damn it. How am I going to eat?

He has to avoid another bout of publicity over drugs. Not another rehab. Can't let anyone know he's been using. He'll go cold turkey this time. He's done it before. He's quit several times, cold turkey, on his own, suffered, yes, but showed he has the fortitude to do it. But something always intervenes, career failure, relationship failure, and he'll be right back on. He's had the rehab experience time and time again. Contingent with his signature on a motion-picture contract, he will lick it again. In Hollywood, his drug use always falls to zero upon receipt of a massive infusion of funds.

Years ago, he'd collaborated on a screenplay, creating a role for himself that had won him an Academy Award for Best Actor. In that role, Jim had borrowed his true-life propensity for violence. In the Jeep, the violent Horse had been borrowing energy and vibes from Jim.

That had been another secret that had gotten out a few years ago. Jim's impulsive violence had led to loss of standing in Hollywood. His original screenplays all seemed the same: violence along the lines of what Jim did in real life. No one seemed to be interested—except that one time.

This time it was no different. He was playing himself again, though with a twist. The double murder he and Horse had reenacted paralleled an actual murder case of thirty years ago in which a real person named Clark Holcomb had picked up a real hitchhiker named Daniel Lends His Horse, both dying several hours later and hundreds of miles away in a Canadian farm field of knife wounds inflicted during an apparent fight to the death.

The saga of Clark and Horse had been a brief news story from Jim's childhood, a scratch on his memory. No one knew the real story behind it, so he was able to approach it with a degree of flexibility that had been absent in his prior collaborations. Now he had to secure a contract, get someone to cut a check, and begin the screenplay.

Mirror time. He replenishes the hand basin with sterile water from downstairs, positions the dresser mirror to catch driblets of sun, and pulls the suture pack from the first-aid kit he'd brought in from the Jeep. He holds the suture needle in the jaws of the needle driver and brings the edges of his upper lip wound together. He pushes the needle through the midpoint of the wound with a soft rotating motion, pulls it through, and ties off the suture with a square knot.

While putting in this first suture, he almost got a sense of himself disappearing; it was such a strange thing to be doing to oneself. On impulse, he becomes like a bat swerving through the forest, navigating by echolocation. He goes back to work, distancing himself from the activity. It is someone else, not him. Someone else's wounds, not his. He puts in sutures above and below the first suture until his upper lip wound is held together, but not too tight, allowing room for further swelling. He sutures the lower lip in a similar manner. He is good at this, doesn't know where he picked it up, the instruments tumbling artfully in his hands, fingers doing just exactly as they should, popping needle through flesh again and again, the pain of each pop bearing well.

Finished, he dabs blood from the needle holes, applies first-aid cream, and sticks on sterile bandages. He'll replace the bandages every day and remove the sutures in four days. Pill time again? No, he resists the impulse, still testing his resolve.

He finds the handkerchief he'd used to stanch the flow of blood from his lips and the washcloth he'd used initially to mop his lips with water before discovering that running water up to his face in cupped hands worked better. When Horse cut him in the Jeep, his lips had bled like planets quaking in the springtime of their youth. Both handkerchief and washcloth are filthy with dried blood, dirt, and organic bits of the field. Jim is also filthy, bloody, and dirty from his wounds and the field. He tosses the handkerchief and washcloth into a corner, grabs a clean washcloth, and begins cleaning himself, dipping it in the hand basin. He'll replenish the water, use a little soap, get himself clean, then get fresh clothes from the Jeep.

As he works, a chain of molecules drops in his brain and sudden knowledge comes to him. He knows what the next step in human evolution will be: humans creating things in the manner of gods. Nothing else so inflames the mind. More molecules drop, and he has a sense of losing things and gaining things. Gravity seems stable, but all else is up for grabs.

He forces himself to focus on his immediate concerns. His three thoracic puncture wounds stand bare in the dim, tangled light of the mirror, dull aches interspersed by occasional deep stabs of pain. The wounds were too deep for him to probe and clean thoroughly. But something tells him not to worry. A song runs through him. Black needs white and white needs black. Time needs spiders weaving webs. He decides he will leave it at that.

Window time. Light shoots into his eyes: sharp images of a face in the western sky among the red-tinged clouds, a fierce feline face with eyes that seem to be looking right at him. It fades in and out. He sees it again and again, the artistic lines of face, head, and body. The sight chills him, the alien presence too much for his mind. A molecule drops, and the presence creeps closer, its tail swishing across the floor.

Jim walks downstairs. He and Horse had agreed to isolate themselves until the next morning, when they'd listen to the audio tapes from the murder reenactment and discuss doing a screenplay. Nothing, really, had gone according to plan. And that was okay. They had planned on using a wooden knife with a chalked blade so they could delineate wounds, but Horse had shown up at the cabin with a real knife, which created real wounds. Damn it! Horse knew Jim had gone elk hunting in Montana. He knew Vinita was real.

He walks past Horse's room on the first floor and hears a voice.

"In Peshawar, Pakistan, two Americans amble down a narrow street, looking into merchants' stalls. Amulets, fetishes, potions, and an improbable collection of dead creatures draw their attention and soon they forget their caution. In one of the stalls, a merchant threatens to break all their bones and hang their carcasses from hooks."

It is Horse's voice recording a tale on tape. Something must have struck his fancy during the night. That's okay.

Outside, he circles the Jeep, and then walks to the field and sees the bloody outlines where he and Horse had died. He picks up their gore-filled shirts and looks at the sky. In the east, the atmosphere is growing increasingly dark. In the west, the cloud faces are frozen in huge pink swirls.

Does anyone live here?

Jim turns around. A voice? Horse? No. Wind in the trees at the edge of the field. He looks at the sky again. The face is there, big artistic lines going in and out of focus. Is it a face giving guidance? If so, what kind of guidance?

"Get me my magical elk," he says aloud, memories stirring. He thinks of Vinita. She is real. Horse knows her. He'll go in the house and talk to Horse. Horse will tell him Vinita is real.

He throws their bloody shirts into the back of the Jeep and enters the house, where a heavy smell stops him. He has no reference for it. Has he smelled this before? He walks toward the room where he'd heard the voice and realizes he can't go in there.

Horse's voice comes from the room again, a recording.

"He was a plastic surgeon from California and was recently in Lahore, Pakistan, where he performed several operations to save women's faces. In Pakistan, it is not uncommon for a man to cut his wife's nose off, to burn her face, to disfigure her with knives or acid. The law does not intervene—these are private matters between a Muslim husband and wife. Meanwhile, in the merchant's stall, the two Americans see fish and seahorses and small animals they can't identify. Everything is dead and hanging on hooks. 'For rituals,' the woman says. She has a habit of enlightening him, but she is nervous now, and she leads him away from the stall."

Jim stops midway up the stairs, his hand on the banister. He doesn't like the smell or the darkness or what is taking place down below. It sounds like Horse is working on a new screenplay, burning his way through their supply of batteries for the tape recorder. With no power in the house, they have positioned flashlights in prearranged locations. One waits for him at the head of the stairs. He goes up, grabs it, stands in the darkness. What is Horse doing? He hears the voice from down below.

"His skill as a plastic surgeon is in demand worldwide. His focus is on birth defects that arise out of Third World squalor. He has salvaged lives by giving new appearance and function to faces and limbs. Many of his patients had been hidden away since birth, to save them from death decrees pronounced by ruling clerics. These were the men who decided what was acceptable to God, who lived, who died."

Jim walks into the bedroom, his hope of doing a screenplay with Horse on the old Canadian double homicide now hanging on the meanest of hooks, for it sounds like Horse is working on a screenplay that would overwhelm anything arising out of the confrontation between Clark Holcomb and Daniel Lends His Horse. Whatever was hot in Horse's mind, Horse went with.

He bounces the spot of light around the room. There is no bed. They are roughing it. He'll lie on a sleeping bag he'd brought in earlier. He is still shirtless. He'd forgotten to bring in clean clothes.

Window time. He is a pair of eyes staring out the upper-floor window of the farmhouse. Bare torso. Recovering as if from a death blow to the head. Blink and blink again. What happened? Real? Unreal? He backs away from the window. Avoid mirror. He seems enveloped in a new order, something come to rescue him, probably from some long-forgotten script he'd penned long ago. Something mind-bending and ugly.

This thing that has come to rescue him wants Jim to act in a way contrary to his philosophy and ethics. It wants him to change himself. Not change as in transformation owing to new learning or experience; not change through persuasion or influence; not even change through pressure or coercion, which is ugly enough. No, it is quite different from all that. It wants Jim to change himself by destroying his every molecule of intention and substituting someone else's.

Mirror time. He sees no image, the sky no longer watching him. Night as you like it: dark, no surprises. The day has gone by. He feels broken. He thinks of mothers, his own included, who are equally broken. Mothers who reinforce strange rules for their children, such as teaching them to obey. Obey whom? The enemy? Those who sought to destroy you? Why were children being so hindered? Get a clue. Better to go out disobedient. In the end, it was all disobedience anyway. No one knew anything.

He backs away from the mirror, something tricky fooling him. His whole society has vanished and he is clinging to threads. When the change happens at subtle levels, no one knows they're dead.

He hears the voice from downstairs.

"Muhammad is lacking a left eye socket. There is nothing there. No eye, nothing. Muhammad's left eye is at the end of a pendulous stalk of tissue that grows from his left cheekbone. It is a fully functioning eye; it peers about and has normal vision. When the woman describes Muhammad's condition to the doctor, he says he has read of such cases. She tells him the mullahs pronounce a death sentence when they learn a baby has been born with this condition. Those that survive into adulthood have been hidden away since birth. He nods as she speaks. He understands. Muhammad has spent his life in darkness."

The heavy smell returns to Jim, but now he has a reference for it. It is a rich combination of wood, leather, and horses, and the dusty hot summer street of a small American town from long ago. A carnival-like atmosphere prevails as teams of horses pull circus wagons down the street to the accompaniment of a pipe organ and the delight of an amused citizenry. He can't see the circus procession but knows it is there, and he knows it goes on forever.

Window time. He knows he must look at the dark side of the circus, for along with pipe organs, horses, and clowns, there are tigers.

He needs this screenplay. It would mean another escape from drugs. It would mean not becoming homeless, not having to search for a job. What could he do? Wash dishes? Data entry?

He laughs. His lip wounds tug at the sutures. He shrieks, puts a hand to his mouth, quietening his pain. Mad at himself, he lifts his hand and looks in the mirror, shining the flashlight. There is no blood seeping through the bandages. The sutures had held. Good job, doctor. He could always hang up a shingle. Another way he could go to prison.

Damn it! He isn't going to work at something menial. He has no skills, except writing and acting, and he'd blown them long ago by staying one-dimensional, with a focus on his own real-life violence. And when that didn't work anymore, he'd run out of stories.

Now there was this old double homicide, one of the strangest crimes ever, and no one had ever heard of it. It would work. He'd gotten into it viscerally: blood, guts, emotion. The bedrock of story. He could do this one. It fit his one-dimensional skill set: emotion-driven violence with a twist. All that was left was to persuade Horse to make the movie and sign him for the screenplay.

But he will have to leave Horse to his other screenplay first, for it sounds infinitely better. And maybe later they can work together on the double homicide. Jim is good for that.

He won't go crawling to Horse. Horse wouldn't respect that. Jim won't explain his financial situation to him, how close he is to being homeless. Without anything. He won't tell him he is one step away from falsifying assets to secure a loan—a perfect way to draw the attention of the FBI. Horse wouldn't be impressed.

Jim will find something else to hold over him.

Damn it!

He sees it all unfolding before him. If he returns to L.A. without a contract, his drug use will quadruple; he will go into a bank, lie his way into a loan, and place himself in legal jeopardy. With a contract from Horse, there'll be no more drugs and no more worries. He'll be writing a screenplay. He'll be in his violent element, one approved by society. With no contract, he'll go under. Finished.

No, he won't find something to hold over Horse. He will take the high road. He'll get another visitor in the night up at the cabin. Katrina or Rory or Renée will come and visit. A new story will gel.

He will put Horse in his jaws and make him do this movie if he has to. If it were the only option. But it's not the only option. He has to be careful though. Show no fangs. Keep the fangs invisible. Don't appear too eager. Be inscrutable. Be like the tiger. Be death.

No. He could not do that.

He is ready to go to bed. He walks around the bedroom, his feet creaking on the floorboards, the flashlight showing him the way. He is amazed the sutures held when he laughed. He'll laughed hard sometime. What then? The sutures are almost like a gag. He thinks they will curtail his act somewhat. Maybe not. Maybe they will be a blessing.

He directs the flashlight around, stares at the wood floor and the wood ceiling. Dust in the air, a column of it, smelling it, a hard hit of dust. Dust motes in flux, a wind stirred up. He'd moved his hand, hadn't he? Something moved. He wonders if the dust has any medicinal qualities, hallucinogenic qualities?

Mirror time. He clicks his flashlight off, sees nothing. He feels relief at his physical power and size, for he can sweep Horse up in a bear hug if he likes and crush him. He'll have to get him from behind, though, for Horse has extensive martial arts training. From the front, Horse can kill you. From behind, if he can pin Horse's arms, he can kill Horse. He'll take him from behind, or use the gun, load it with live rounds instead of blanks this time. He'll hold all options in reserve. If he has to kill Horse it will be self-defense. He has the wounds to prove it. He has the tapes they'd made in the Jeep. Before patching his knife wounds, he'd snapped pictures of them remotely on a timer. The raw wounds on his torso and lips. He'd done it to record realistic details, but now the photos served another purpose.

If he kills Horse, it has to be soon, somewhere down the road they'll follow in the morning. It won't be ruled murder, though, not with what Horse did to him. Multiple knife wounds, the taped voices. Doing the screenplay is what he prefers. The tiger behind the bushes is in reserve. At some level, he has to make sure Horse knows the tiger is there.

A self-possessed voice shakes forth from downstairs.

"They quickly run into a problem. Muhammad is afraid he will lose vision in his left eye if he undergoes surgery. 'No, you will not lose vision,' the doctor tells him. They know the surgery carries risks. Muhammad could wake up blind in his left eye. How can they adequately convey the risks to him? They try. Muhammad agrees to the surgery. They leave, promising to contact him again. They stand at the top of the stairs and quietly discuss the logistics of spiriting Muhammad away from Peshawar for surgery somewhere in the West. It will be a daunting task."

Window time. Jim is a pair of eyes staring from the upper-floor bedroom window, the sun sunk below the horizon. Real? Unreal? He has to get Horse excited about the double homicide again. He needs that contract. He backs away from the window, moves toward the sleeping bag. The script about the plastic surgeon in Peshawar, Pakistan, sounds like it will overwhelm anything else that might enter anyone's mind over the next few months. Jim is sick. But he has an option he never had before. He can change Horse. Kill Horse in some way. When he gets into the sleeping bag, exhaustion takes him over, and in seconds he falls asleep.

⧖

Horse lies in the field and sees the soldiers run in with the poles and posthole digger. They hang his body and Jim's. Later, Horse finds himself wandering.

Horse with his shirt off is at the Jeep and sees two bloody shirts in the back. He seems to have a helper beside him, someone intoxicated on the idea of writing up the double homicide and making money. Horse is now showered and dressed and in the downstairs bedroom of the farmhouse, hearing noises upstairs, talk of Vinita.

He recalls Vinita: soft, sensuous, like an enchanted princess from a fairy tale. Horse is shaken out of his role: stumbling, arcing across the heavens, a large face upon the world, the farmhouse small below him, the whole world small. Horse is in the house again, in the living room. No, he can't call anyone or speak to anyone. He and Jim have an agreement: They won't discuss any of this until tomorrow. Their conversations in the Jeep are on tape, the tape machine now in the corner of the first-floor bedroom. They'll go to work on it tomorrow. In a few days he'll know if he has a movie and if he wants another working relationship with Jim. Jim had been unbelievable as Clark Holcomb. If they make the movie, he wonders who they can get to play Lends His Horse.

Something bothers Horse. He has to keep reminding himself he is not Horse. The role had been so vivid. The whole thing somehow got tangled in his mind. He had no script worked out, played it entirely by ear. Am I a philosopher? Weird. Something else is bothering him. When Jim mentioned Vinita Scoggins, he knew her. He'd been with her in Montana.

Did their minds blend on this? They'll have to talk about Vinita tomorrow. Is this project meant to be, then, since they'd blended so well on Vinita? No, it didn't work that way.

"Get me my magical elk."

He hears this from Jim upstairs. He smiles. Shut up, Jim. It's not yet time for us to talk about it. Let it rest.

He rummages around, makes noise, has to for some reason, doesn't know why, Jim walking down the stairs, Horse having to mask something, can't let him walk in here, see me. Why? No mirror in here. Mirror upstairs. None here. Stay away, Jim, don't enter, our agreement. We'll discuss it tomorrow.

Sounds fading, the person going out the door. Horse thinks he busied himself for another reason—he wasn't supposed to creep to the doorway and take a look at this person passing by. He wasn't supposed to see who walked out the door. Now he has to wait. Will the person walk back in? Yes. And he'll have to do more busy work, to keep himself from taking a peek.

Jim returns to the farmhouse and Horse hears him walk upstairs. Sounds fade. Phew. Over. Tomorrow. He crawls on top of his open sleeping bag, shirtless. He'll put on a shirt in the morning. Can't find one right now. His left side from the foot up is constricting his movements.

He has ideas on the movie. He doesn't think it will work unless a major new plot element is injected. Someone has to survive the deaths of Clark and Horse. The story has to be about someone else. Who? Vinita? She's the logical choice. And what would her role be? He'll ask her. What am I thinking? Vinita isn't real. Yes, she is. Horse is in her house, floating around. No, just tired. Need to sleep.

Later in the night, Horse hears Jim's voice from the doorway of his bedroom, speaking to him. Can't be. Jim is upstairs, asleep. They have this agreement. They don't want to confuse anything tonight. They'll let it settle and discuss it in the morning.

Horse goes to the doorway with a flashlight, his left side dragging. No Jim there. He goes to the window, pulls it open, stares out. Vinita in the sky, face upon the world, wherever you are, come here. Meet us in this place. Give this story a chance. Vinita is like oceans in flux, storms in heaven.

California in a Bottle. It was Jim's Academy Award winning role. Horse and Jim had written the screenplay. It was right here, in his mind. Thinking of Las Vegas. The rip-off crew. Jim an innocent victim. Losing big money in a swindle. If he'd had a gun, three dead punks. Rage. How to channel it? Destroy them. Kill the three punks. Horse would have their scalps.

Jim had told him how he spent several months stalking the three. For real, with a gun. How he kept himself in check, never killing them. They'd made a movie, Horse borrowing Jim's rage. It had won Jim best actor. He owed Jim. He'd try to make this nasty piece of work, this double homicide on the prairie, into a movie. The three Nevada punks became a metaphor for everything. In the end, the three were insignificant, not worth killing. And the would-be killer had found himself, what he truly was. It made all the difference, this catalyst. This rage. Then stopping it upon seeing the antlike vermin for what they were. Bigger things awaited.

Horse goes back to sleep. Vinita is in his dreams, but she will not let him come close. He reaches for her again and again, but she is a will-o'-the-wisp in the starry sky, and his arms enclose nothing. He watches her soar, another star gone up and away, twinkling in the starry night.

He wakes, his pulse pounding, his eyes stinging, his heart in a tight grip. In Peshawar, Pakistan, Vinita took him to see Muhammad, a man with an eye on a stalk who had spent his entire life in darkness. Vinita, the wily, cool brunette, had entered his life with all the madness of a dream, her last, lingering touch still fresh on his fingertips.

Now he tries to sleep again.

Three

⧗ THE ELK HUNT ⧗

Jim Lasher waited until he saw the bull elk's breath, waited some more until he saw a wary lift of head, and then a twitch of attention. The elk was sprung tight, about to blow into dramatics. Jim stood in a thicket on a chilly Montana hillside watching an elk herd maneuver uphill. He drew a bead, squeezed the trigger, felt the explosion as the bullet left the barrel on a trajectory into the kill zone. The bull dropped, its final breath a ghostly presence above its head. The rest of the herd crashed through the woods, frantic hoofbeats tearing apart the tranquilly of the morning.

Jim heard a volley of shots downhill, but didn't think his hunting companions hit anything except black earth and pine forest. The kill he had worked so hard for was over and done with, and he felt relieved. He'd been worried he'd leave Montana and return to Los Angeles without a kill.

As he walked from concealment, he had powerful thoughts of donating the meat to a local family in need. His wife, Renée, had been telling him they should be more giving. *It's the greatest feeling you'll ever get, Jim,* she would say. *Giving selflessly creates its own special kind of reward.* When his hunting companions joined him, he asked them if they knew of a family in the area that could use the meat. One of them said he knew of a family named Scoggins that lived on a small farm tucked into the hills.

"They're from some foreign place, Jim. They're upright folks. But beware. The old timers around here say magic has been practiced in these hills for ages. Some of it is related to the earth and animals. Some of it is Old-World magic that the pioneers and settlers brought with them. Witchcraft and sorcery, that type of thing. Some practice it for protection. Some with evil intent. Strange goings-on are reported. The Scoggins are good 'uns, though. They'll take in charity. Give them your kill."

When Jim drove up to the Scoggins' farmstead with the elk draped across the hood of his Jeep, four people rushed out to greet him. In a flurry of activity, they untied the carcass, dropped it off the hood, and stepped back. A girl about nineteen with long dark hair and a slender figure told him thanks. Jim could not take his eyes off her. She was like a silk breeze from China. An old man kept shifting his gaze between the elk and Jim, appraising both. Two hulking boys hung behind the old man. Jim was hoping the old man would ask him in. He wondered how easy it would be to take the girl to bed. The girl's eyes began laughing. She said thanks again.

Jim nodded, but he was not through. He introduced himself and asked their names. The old man said his name was Raphael Scoggins. He said the girl was Vinita Scoggins and the boys were Tory and Angelo Scoggins. After this name-sharing, Raphael asked Jim in, and they all sat at the kitchen table and drank dark apple cider and told tales of the woods and animals and hunting. And then they went out and butchered the elk.

Jim said he would like to return to the Scoggins' Montana home. Raphael said he'd be welcome. Jim returned three times that fall and winter, twice in spring, and twice in summer.

He and Vinita had French toast and coffee at the kitchen table on a morning after he had spent the night in her bed. Smells of incense, spice, candles, and rich mahogany roamed the house. A touch of satin was everywhere. Jim had bought Raphael a Ford pickup truck, Vinita a Ford Explorer, and Tory and Angelo mountain bikes. He had given them money besides, helping them start savings and investment accounts.

Jim believed Raphael and Vinita knew right off his intentions. He believed invisible sparks flew when he killed the elk and that an agreement had been struck in low earth. Renée noticed money disappearing from their bank accounts and was ecstatic, for she thought her husband was accomplishing worthy aims.

But her husband had disappeared from the map. Her husband wondered what weakness of character had led him into this orbit, what cosmic torment awaited him. Renée's hardworking, steady spouse knew he would not get away unscathed.

Jim made his retreat from silky Vinita Scoggins that summer morning, promising to return in another month or so. Vinita's parting words made everything different. They were like big footprints on the earth.

"Jim, I've been meaning to tell you something."

"Oh, what's that?"

"A catastrophic event killed us all. We are all dead, and we are not used to being dead. That is why we are having tricks played on our minds."

"Where'd you hear that?"

"Ideas are floating around; the most powerful one is that we are all dead."

"When did this event happen?"

"No one knows."

Four

⧗ THE CAR TRIP ⧗

In southwestern North Dakota, when Jim stopped for fuel, gusts flattened the fields along I94 and a lick of moisture splashed his eye as he stepped from the Jeep. He paid with a credit card at the pump, inserted the nozzle, squeezed the lever, and felt the rush of gasoline into the Jeep's fuel tank. His palm had grown icy cold from the flow when a man in a worn buckskin shirt and blue jeans ambled up to him.

"I need a ride. I can help pay for gas."

The man had some kind of disability on the left side of his body, most apparent in his gait, which seemed not as springy and free compared to his right side. His voice was brisk, deep, the cadence too abrupt for polite conversation. Something eager lay about him, like he'd just run from a fight in a dark alley where he'd thumped someone. His long, dark hair framed angular features which flung off auras of intensity and toughness. His eyes were unsettled pools. He yanked two items from his wallet and thrust them at Jim.

Jim jolted fully awake from his long drive at the sight of the intruder. His energy shot skyward as he took the two items in hand and held them up so he could read them and track the man at the same time.

He saw an Indian tribal ID encased in cracked plastic and a letter from a tribal police agency dated a week ago. Both ID and letter said the man's name was Daniel Lends His Horse. The letter pulled no punches; it said the man Horse was traveling to Grand Forks to see about attending the University of North Dakota; it said there were no outstanding arrest warrants pending on Horse; it said Horse had never been convicted of a felony. The whole thing looked fishy to Jim.

With one hand still holding the icy nozzle grip, Jim returned the ID and letter to Horse. He looked the man over. Horse's buckskin shirt was open to mid-chest, the flesh bare, bronzed, chiseled. His eyes looked hard, but softened when he saw he was being studied.

Jim felt a need to protect his flank. He looked around, watched the weather grow fuzzy. As soon as the tank was full, he planned on jumping into the Jeep and taking off down I94. He planned on putting as much distance between himself and Lends His Horse as he possibly could. Jim believed the criminal-justice system had long ago collapsed into a strange circus that had vultures as the only paying customers. The manner in which Lends His Horse chose to advertise himself did not engender any great confidence in this system.

Horse held his arms up as if invoking the gods.

"When is this sky going to give us our downpour?"

Jim saw big raindrops hit the asphalt beyond the roof that protected the fuel islands, heard the plunk grow rhythmic. He thought it was way too dangerous to pick up a hitchhiker.

"What are you going to take up in college?"

"I'm thinking English. I'm thinking philosophy." Horse held his lips close together when he talked, the words coming from deep in his throat.

"Oh?" Jim had spent one year at the University of Kansas before transferring to UCLA. He'd entertained similar ideas as Lends His Horse before psychology and neuroscience had begun a powerful pull on him.

"I had those kinds of thoughts at one time. Have you ever considered medicine or perhaps psychology or neuroscience?"

"Yes, I have. But I am better suited for English and philosophy. I have questions, though, about college teachers. I hear they can make it rough or easy."

"Which do you prefer?"

"Neither. I prefer honesty. I hear some teachers are bitches."

"There are bitches all over the place. God sprinkles them in. Anywhere you care to lay down tracks."

"You're right."

The Jeep's tank was full. Jim removed the nozzle and stuck it back in the pump. He'd been assessing the physical prowess of Horse, but also breaking him down in terms of animal instincts. Anything could be approached as if it were an animal that needed bringing down. He thought he glimpsed a knife on Horse's belt. There was something there, hidden by the buckskin shirt.

"Let me see your knife. I know knives."

Horse took a step toward him, a gait like a snapping whip,

his eyes tight little eagle's eyes, his mouth a tight little snake's mouth.

"You're seeing a woman," Horse said, "a perky one. I can tell. The last ride I accepted, I won't tell what happened. That's why I carry this knife. How's that woman you've been seeing?"

Horse offered the knife haft-first to Jim.

Jim took the knife in hand. The blade was doglegged, ax-thick on its back edge, razor-sharp on its cutting edge.

"You want to hear my philosophy on women?" Horse asked.

"No."

Jim knew his knives, but the saga on this one was fractured in various parts of his mind. He thought it was Asian, a work tool and a weapon.

"What do you know about this knife?" he asked Horse.

"I know volumes about the knife. No doubt you've been seeing a woman. Not your wife, I'd wager. I didn't mean to scare you."

"I wasn't scared."

"Don't hold back on me. I know you've been seeing a woman. I'll tell you my philosophy on women."

"I'd rather not hear it." Jim grabbed the Jeep's door handle. But what was he going to do with this knife? He couldn't give it back to Horse. That would make him some kind of accessory, wouldn't it, if Horse used it to commit a crime? And he couldn't keep it—that would be stealing. He decided he would stall and think of a way out.

"How much do you want for this knife?"

"First, tell me what I call you?"

"Jim."

"First name? Last name?"

"Jim is my first name. Lasher is my last name."

"See? You sound more responsible when you use simple, well-organized language. Call me Horse. It's simpler than Lends His Horse. It's more concise and elegant than Daniel. It's your wife you've been seeing. Right? I knew it? What's her name?"

"Horse, this knife almost looks homemade."

"It is homemade, if you call a factory in someone's back-yard homemade."

Horse took the knife from Jim and held it up. "In war, the sight of this knife has been known to scare people into sur-rendering."

Horse put the knife back in its sheath.

"I have a philosophy on women. What's your wife's name?"

"Renée."

"Is there a problem in your marriage? You have one. Are you working on it?"

"Renée is too much of a support person for too many people. She doesn't see it as a problem, though."

"What kind of animals do you hunt?"

"How'd you know I hunt?"

"I saw your gear through the Jeep's windows."

"Elk, moose, black bear, mountain lion."

"Each of them dangerous. What motivates you to hunt?"

"It's the challenge of setting out to do something and bringing about a result. You can do that in many areas in life, but with hunting, you are out in the elements, and you have a wild creature that still follows its instincts. You have to be alert to everything, to the terrain, to the weather, to the wind direction, to the animals' feeding habits. Only then are you likely to have a successful hunt."

"Jim, did you hunt Renée? Or did she just happen along?"

"Uh, she was just there, in school, at UCLA. She worked in a law office part time. I needed some legal work done. I'd appeared in a motion picture; something sticky was taking place and I needed advice. We kind of fell in together."

"Ah, you should hunt your woman."

"I can't hunt for Renée."

"Why not?"

"She's not an animal. Her instincts are all wrong. She's not hard to find. She's way too predictable."

"She has undiscovered territory. Try hunting her. A strange thought, isn't it? It's the essence of my philosophy. Is there something of Renée in the spaces between things? Does something of Renée permeate things? Is she lost in glacial crevasses? Are parts of Renée held in dark places? This is metaphysical."

"It is."

"You're going to hunt for Renée in all the unlikely places you'd never before thought of looking. How's that?"

"That's strange."

"It is, but I base the hunt on a metaphysical idea: Renée, your wife, is everywhere, but we normally see her only within the package we call Renée. The hunt for Renée involves searching for the animal essence that moves swiftly all around us. We call this the swift land animal. And in fact, we are all swift land animals."

"Horse, have you been smoking hash? Is that what you use that knife for, to chop hashish?"

"You're sidetracking me. We are everywhere, but the most diminished part of us is probably right here, in this world.

What you can see. Like my poor brother Melvyn. He was a cop. A California cop. Gunned down in the line of duty. Paralyzed. Somewhere, Melvyn is whole."

"Horse, I had no idea."

"Jim, it's a kukri knife, used by Nepalese tribesmen. The British Army recruited them to serve in special combat units. During World War II, the tribesmen, called Gurkhas, were deployed on nighttime beheading missions behind German lines. Do I get in the Jeep now?"

Something was telling Jim to let Horse in the Jeep. It would be all right. He reasoned he could take Horse in a fight if he really had to. The best defense in a knife fight was to control the arm that wielded the knife. Horse's left side was unwieldy. He'd be up against a man who was practically one-armed. Watch the right arm. If it made a move, attack it.

Jim experienced a whole-body shudder. It was happening again. He was being led into something not of his own making. This was like the first time he entered the Scoggins' home. An intimation of danger unsettling him. He was determined to discover the origin of this process, how people did this to him, and turn it around.

Jim saw Horse eyeing another car that had just pulled up to the pumps, a family with young children. This clarified his decision: He'd have to take Horse, or he might finagle a ride with someone more vulnerable. Jim wanted to go see Vinita again right away after this, or go home and tell Renée everything. He thought Horse could help him choose. Horse seemed to be his vehicle for the moment. A philosopher-savant. Dangerous to the core.

"You get in the Jeep."

Like that, Horse had his leash on him. Jim was always susceptible to the one with charisma. His wife did it to him. Vinita did it to him. Snap a leash on. Hunting was his one way to slip the leash. Seeing Horse enter the Jeep, he knew another hunt was on.

⌛

Hour after hour, an armada of heat-thrashing storms floated over the prairie, grazing the land with explosive electrical strikes and drenching rain; in the intervals, sunlight baked the earth nearly dry before the next cloudburst. Ahead through the Jeep's windshield, Jim glimpsed a trio of ducks floating in a patch of ditch water, green heads reflecting the sunlight. It was another odd bit of nature that would not last out the day.

"Horse, look, ducks in the ditch."

Horse moved in his seat like a lasso fell around his torso and yanked him upright. He had a repertoire of such moves, none of them likely learned at the hands of a physical therapist. He squinted out the windshield and chuckled at the ducks. Horse would sometimes laugh at his own physical asymmetry—it was obvious he was having difficulty; he'd told Jim the left side of his body from the foot up felt like clay, yet outside the Jeep he'd seemed so ungodly quick and strong. How come? Did a power sometimes come over him?

As Horse turned to watch the duck flotilla pass by, Jim cast his eyes in search of Horse's knife. It was in the same place, on his belt, concealed by the buckskin shirt. As Horse jacked forward, Jim shot his eyes back to the road. Early on, Horse had told him he didn't care to have sloppy eyes fall on him.

Don't like to be spied on, Jim. Do you? Horse had drawn his knife then, as if to emphasize the point.

"Funny thing those ducks," Horse said, his eyes leaving smoke trails around the Jeep's interior. "They have no idea they're someone's lunch. Guess they're not much different than humans in that regard." His knife was in hand. Jim hadn't seen him draw it. He slid a thumbnail along the long, sharp edge. "It's always war, Jim. For ducks. For us. Not many know it."

At the sound of Horse's voice, the harmonics of the highway began whipping through Jim, resonating in all the little rivulets of mind and body—the din of engine, the strum of tires, the flail of wind. He imagined he was in the back of a troop carrier, going into battle, enveloped in a cocoon of heat, dust, and oil. He felt a tingling sensation all over and knew he was picking up the beginning cadences of war. Sooner or later it would be just a rhythm. A beat of war drums.

Jim sighed and saw brush strokes from God and was touched by a universe that knew war and did war and knew and did nothing else, a blind and stumbling universe with its face rigid upon war.

"War is beguiling, Jim, for it makes you do something; it makes you search for your real self. If you are real, you do not stand still while some motherfucker shoves a hot poker up your ass—you kill the motherfucker. A highly conditioned human will stand still and do nothing."

Horse sheathed his knife.

"Have you seen the underside of a rainforest canopy, Jim? It seals off the upper reaches where sunlight stabs the world. From inside your own little world, when it rains, you see water drip down from the canopy to the understory and ground.

No one on the ground is the wiser, no one knows how much it rained above the canopy or how much sunlight hit it; they only know their own little part of the world, which is very limited. They have no knowledge of the origin of the things that sustain them. They are shielded from this higher knowledge, and that is a metaphor for so much. So much is hidden from ordinary lives. Does that help to clarify your situation?"

"It does." After listening to Horse for several hours, Jim had no further illusions. He would go see Vinita Scoggins again as soon as he could; he'd never tell Renée what he had become. The search for the origin of how people were able to slip a leash on him lay on the far side of Vinita. Of this he was sure. He thought of Horse as something of his savior.

"Those dark clouds flanking us are holding back a torrent from hell," Horse said, looking at the sky. "Let's see if we can outrun them. You need to keep your eyes on the road."

"Horse, I'm driving safe." He didn't care for Horse's instructions. "A person gets too entranced with constant attention on the road." It was as if the man had never been behind the wheel. He glanced at the sky, the skin on the back of his neck prickling.

"Jim, why is it something tells me that if I attend this university up here there's going to be someone, probably an old lady, that will attack me with arrogant, pseudo-intellectual bullshit remarks the fuckholes are using these days to control zombie fucks like me they pull off the shelf to stock their classrooms with, and they won't ever be from around these parts; they'll be from some other place, maybe from a prestigious university where they sucked ass and got a degree and now they're unfit for anything except lying to you and tying you down and raping you where you can't fight back; their life is over since they can't do anything else, so they have to kill you. Tell me, you've been there. Why is there something telling me that? Why is there something telling me I'm going to be assaulted if I go to school there, probably assaulted regularly, and the situation will be that if I fight back they'll destroy me, cause those are the rules? Why is it I'm required to be polite and responsible but they can be evil any which way they want? They're inferior; I'm not. At least I don't think so. All I want is honesty and responsibility from them. Why is something telling me that's exactly what I won't get, but will get fucked instead, probably by an old lady who's fucked up enough so she'll never get fired and has lots of dumb fuckers sucking her ass?"

"It can happen anywhere, Horse. Not just here in your part of the world, but anywhere."

Horse pulled his knife and slid his thumbnail along the sharp edge. "The Gurkhas snuck behind German lines and beheaded unsuspecting enemy. Tell me what to do at school, Jim. I'm concerned."

"Get your legal house in order, Horse. Teachers like the one you mentioned are bound to be scared some student is going to turn them in. Make that your reputation. Know how to report a teacher's bad behavior before you enter a classroom the first time. Never reveal yourself to them. Watch it if they ask personal questions. They own you if they know you too well; it opens up avenues of attack. Make note of any personal questions they ask and turn them in. Always be thinking of the rules they must follow. Make sure the school enforces those rules or else you'll be taken advantage of."

"Why is it they say I'm a bad student, Jim? Why don't they say I have bad teachers? They've got you where they want you. They harass you and if you respond in a self-respecting way, you get arrested. Tell me why."

"The world is fucked, Horse. See? Now you've got me talking that way. Really, only some of them are bad."

"Oh, really? How am I going to pay for this, Jim? Do you have any idea? And if by some miracle I get a degree without having to suck assholes or kill anyone, what am I going to do?"

"You'd need a graduate degree to teach at the university level."

"I knew it. More school. More expense. And then I bet no one would hire me anyway. What am I going to do? I'm a philosopher with no school, no résumé, no future."

"You could kill someone."

Horse snapped upright, like someone jerking his string.

"Really, Jim?"

"No, I'm kidding."

"No, you're not. Why'd you say that?"

"I'm, uh, you ever see that Hitchcock film, *Strangers on a Train?*"

"Yeah, I've seen that one. Two guys meet on a train and negotiate murders. Each kills the other's nemesis. Right?"

"It didn't work out that way, but that's the essence."

"Who do you want me to kill, Jim?"

"Suppose I knew an old broad who had you where she wanted you. She could be any kind of evil, and there was no way you could fight back—the system had you cornered. What would you say to that, if I knew an old broad like that and wanted you to kill her and you knew—"

"And I knew a similar old broad and you'd kill her."

"We'd swap murders. The cops would never know unless one of us talked or we screwed up and left signs of ourselves."

"They'd know. Don't go up against the pros, Jim. Even the dumbest of them can trip us up more ways than we can think of."

"But people do get away with murder."

"They do, but it's a miracle. The only miracle I'm counting on is getting through school without killing anyone, without eating shit, without some old pampered fuck attacking me."

"You won't make it."

"No?"

"Not unless you learn the rules for teachers, enforce the rules, never miss class or an assignment, and never reveal anything of yourself. Keep them guessing; that's your power. Fight them like you've crawled from the seas and it's your mission to create the biosphere. Then you win. You beat the old fucks. The old fucks and young fucks will hate you, but you'll win."

"Now I've got you talking like a philosopher, Jim. You're wise to these phonies. Now I need a job. Got any advice there?"

"No, sorry."

"I'm only good as a philosopher, Jim. I can't do much else. But my philosophy and my way and this knife will get me in trouble doing just about anything. What do you suggest?"

"Can you tone yourself down?"

"No. I'm dead then. I'm gone. Vanished. Tried it. It was forced on me once. They killed me. Now I'm back. This incarnation works only as long as I'm a philosopher. I'm dead otherwise."

"You're older than most other students. They'll be less likely to attack you. They might think you know how to fight back. They like young meat. They devour young meat."

"Now I've got you talking, Jim. You'll be a philosopher yet. Where'd you come from before I hitched on? Montana?"

"Uh, yeah. Montana."

"Hunting?"

"Yes. Hunting."

"You're thinking something, aren't you, Jim? You're thinking I'm not telling you the truth. You're thinking everything I've presented to you is false. Isn't that what you're thinking?"

Horse's voice was low-throated, almost a whisper, like a lion leaning close enough to dip a whisker in Jim's ear.

"I don't know what I'm thinking, Horse."

"Why else would I be here, Jim? Why else would I have hitched a ride with you?"

Horse's breath encircled him, besieged his tear ducts and nostrils with biting insolence. The moisture in Jim's body sought outlets, but there were no outlets. Horse was about to change things on him. But how? And why? He wanted to let Horse out. But it wasn't time; they were still several miles from Grand Forks. Besides, Horse was like his shadow now, a nemesis, but an important one.

He had a thought. Am I Horse? Maybe I can bluff him. I'll tell him I don't think he's real. I'll tell him he's me. An essence that crept out of me because of what I'd been doing in Montana. Because of what I've become. I've conjured this guy Horse.

"Horse, I'm beginning to catch on."

"Oh? How?"

"You might be me, or I might be you. There might be just one of us in this Jeep."

"Whichever one it is, he'd better keep his eyes on the road."

"We're not real."

"We aren't?"

"No, Horse. We aren't. None of this is. I think you've been trailing me since last October."

"I have?"

"Yes. Since the elk hunt in Montana. You came into being then."

"I did?"

"Yes, you did. And for about eight months you were too intangible to evolve physically on this plane. You were like an idea, more or less. And now the time has come for that idea to manifest."

"You're shitting me."

"I'm shitting no one. You've been stalking me because of what I've become. You are me, I am you. We are aspects of the same energy. Savvy?"

"I don't know. What have you become?"

"You know what I've become. It might not be rock solid in your mind right now, but it's in there somewhere, within the field of knowing. Let it come to you."

"You're shitting me."

"Let it come to you. I know we are one and the same. I wanted to give the kill to a needy family. They warned me. They said magic was practiced in those hills. I kept coming back to her, Horse. An exotic girl. You know her?"

"I know her."

"Liar. What's her name?"

Clouds enveloped Horse, and he seemed to vanish, only to reappear like a plane scudding through bad weather.

"*You* tell me her name, Jim."

"You want her bad, don't you?"

Jim saw a road sign. They were seven miles south of Grand Forks. Soon, he'd have to let Horse off. But he didn't want to. Not now. Horse possessed skills. He wanted to know what his game was.

"You're paranoid, Jim. What about the magical elk?"

"What?"

"You said magical elk just now."

"No, I didn't."

"You did. What about this magical elk? You said you gave it to a needy family? What does that symbolize? Who is needier than me? I'm your needy family, Jim. Now you're going to stop somewhere and get me my magical elk. What do you say, Jim? What do you say?"

The change. It was upon him. Jim's breathing stalled. His whole life seemed to go bloodless. This was a holdup.

Horse laughed, and Jim's thoughts wandered thick, new territory. Horse's laughter became a broomstick quickly dancing, and something forced Jim down, a crushing force he couldn't resist; it stole his breath away. Horse's laughter turned the air in the Jeep dungy gray, and became like prison bars, and Jim became filled with terror, bouncing up and down the dungeon stairs, bouncing off the walls and out the tower transom. Horse's laughter died away, and so did Jim. Horse's knife became a gleaming idol in his hand. He had a tidy, focused way about him.

"Keep your eyes on the road."

"All along," Jim said, catching his breath, "I should have known. A holdup."

"Jim, I'm approximately five times as strong as you. And twice as fast. And I've got the knife. Don't try anything."

"You bastard. I knew it. That letter. The ID. Both were fake. You pull this before?"

"Drain your wounds. We've got work to do."

"Get anything from anyone else?"

"Maybe. The magical elk, Jim. Be thinking. That's the only way you'll ever see your sweet-pie Renée again. Or maybe I should say Vinita. Be thinking of how you are going to get me my magical elk. Money, lucre, you know what I mean. Are you thinking?"

"We bypass Grand Forks, then?"

"If need be."

"No point in going there? The university was just a con?"

"You've got it figured, Jim. Magical elk. Be thinking."

Jim's mind was whizzing with ideas, cons, scams—things elastic enough for possibilities.

"Canada."

"Why Canada?"

"I know someone there. A hunting partner."

"We'd have to pass through a border inspection station."

"Horse, this guy's loaded. You could take him for millions. Don't you see? I'm in it with you. I don't even like the guy. He's an old broad, so to speak. He'd tie you down and rape you and make sure the rules prevented you from ever fighting back. He's your philosophical opposite. Mine too. We'll go see him. You'll get your magical elk."

"The border."

"I know."

"The knife will be in your ribs, Jim."

"Yeah, take it easy. We're together now."

"If you say."

"Take it easy."

"I think I'll rip you a new asshole, Jim."

"So rip me a new asshole, why don't you? Go ahead. Who cares?"

"It'll be silent, Jim. Fast and deadly. Right in your ribs."

"Yeah, I know. Hold on. The border."

"Are you sure you know what you're doing, Jim? Is this going to work?"

"I tell you, I hate this guy. *Strangers on a Train.* We'll both kill him, after we con him. You're me, understand? And I'm you. That's what I think."

"If you're shitting me."

"Hold your horses, Horse."

"The border."

"We'll make it. I've got a good feeling this time."

"Watch what you say to the border guards."

"They won't be a problem."

"How far up in Canada?"

"Not far. A farm, Horse. It'll be a farm."

"I'll rip you a new asshole, Jim, stick you in the ribs if this doesn't pan out."

"Don't worry."

"I'll rip you a new asshole, Jim."

"Keep that knife out of sight."

"It'll be in your ribs, Jim."

"If they see it."

"They won't."

"They might. They might look in through the windows. They might ask us to step out."

"I'll play it by ear."

"They'll pull you out if they see it."

"I'm going to rip you a new asshole, Jim."

"Tell me what to do, Horse. You're the philosopher."

"Why should I tell you what to do?"

"I'm faced with a deadly threat."

"Jim, your whole life should have prepared you for this moment. If it hasn't, you and your culture have been negligent. Your life as framed by your culture should have included psychological as well as physical training. The theory is: Overwhelm your senses with chaos and fear and deadly forces that spring at you without warning, and you will do well later when faced with lesser challenges. What we're facing now should actually be a lesser challenge for you, for me, for everyone; but you act as if it's blowing you away. Your eternal soul will not be happy with the results."

"That's warped, Horse. What's my eternal soul got to do with it?"

"When I was younger, I woke one morning with my left heel exploding in pain. I was hobbling something terrible for days. I wasn't much good for anything. I was like some little beast laid low. No one could help me. No one cared. Eventually the pain worked its way up my body and engulfed me, but just on the left side. I would trip to new levels every day. I became known as the fire beast, I was crying so much, like I was trying to put out that fire inside me. You don't see me crying now, do you?"

"No."

"I mastered my life when I realized I'd never get any direction from anyone. The adults in my life were useless fucks; culture creates useless fucks; culture itself was a useless fuck. I stopped crying and convinced myself I was strong and quick. I nudged myself every day and overcame almost everything. I have to keep doing that or I'm dead. You have a condition, too, Jim. But it's not physical like mine. You didn't wake one morning like I did. You woke with a leash on you. You never made a commitment to take it off. Now is your time to take it off. What does your eternal soul have to do with it? It wants you to occasionally act as if you had your leash off."

"You are me. I am you."

"Bullshit. We're discrete individuals. And you have a leash on."

"Tell me what to do. You are me. I am you."

"Jim, you're pathetic. At this stage of your life, you should be as massive and strong as a bull."

"I know, but I'm not."

"You're not. If you were, you could disarm me and break my bones."

"I know, but I can't."

"No, you can't. And you're resigned to your fate."

"No, I'm not. Tell me what to do."

"You're waiting for them to take you away."

"I'm not."

"You are."

"Tell me what to do."

"Sit tight. Don't worry. I'll take you from your cell and lead you to the execution chamber."

"You're ruining my life. You are me, remember?"

"Jim, since we hooked up earlier today, your intellect has lost at least fifty percent of its bone and muscle mass. Pump iron, fucking old whore."

"Horse, I thought you cared. I'm getting farther and farther away from my goal of seeing Vinita again and never telling my wife what I've become and discovering the origin of how people so easily put a leash on me."

"Those are your goals?"

"Yes."

"You'll thank me for ruining your life."

"All along, Horse, you've had me on the most devastating leash of all. And I don't think you're going to let me off it until I'm dead. Maybe not even then."

"You're crying."

"What am I supposed to do?"

"Primp yourself in your chair."

"What?"

"You asked me what you should do. I told you. Primp yourself in your chair."

"Give me something of substance."

"Jim, very soon you should begin to experience the presence of a being. That's my personal interpretation of what is taking place. To me, it's a being. To others, it's a machine. This being or machine is dangerous, for it gives you power. Do you want it?"

"Yes."

"Funny, I think I want it, too. Tell me what that means, Jim?"

"I don't know. I'm scared."

"Oh? What do you plan on doing?"

"I have to act soon."

"But what? And how?"

"Why am I telling you this? I've told you my life's work. Why do I let you do this to me? I've told you too much, Horse."

"Heck, forget it."

"You've yanked my leash for the last time."

"Forget it."

Jim put a hand over his mouth. He couldn't tell Horse anything more. He had to prepare for a physical confrontation. In a knife fight, it was almost certain you'd be cut. You had to minimize the damage, and then control the arm that wielded the knife. It would be Horse's right arm, unless Horse had been bluffing about his disability. Maybe Horse ran an elaborate ruse to lull suckers. But he didn't think so. He thought it was real.

Jim removed his hand from his mouth.

"Horse, you're throwing away your goals of education and career with this move."

He clamped his hand over his mouth again; he didn't trust himself; he assumed Horse still had a leash on him.

"I'm a philosopher. Goals of education and career are secondary. Both are geared to culture, and culture is a useless fuck."

Jim was determined to end it. He would not let Horse walk away from this. But how? It seemed Horse held all the cards.

"Sometimes your philosophy sucks."

Jim clamped his mouth shut. That slipped out. He wouldn't let it happen again. He had another idea. Maybe Horse was putting him on. Maybe this was just another way philosophers had of introducing a problem and then resolving it. How could he find out? Horse was capable of running elaborate bluffs. If he told Horse he'd made up the hunting partner in Canada he could gauge his reaction and learn the truth.

No, he couldn't risk that. Horse had his knife out. He was quick. He was deadly. A philosopher could always think of a way to justify a killing.

Horse yanked Jim's leash.

"Fire beast, you have a question?" Jim asked.

"You been there, Jim?"

"Canada? I've been there."

"Hunting?"

"Yes."

"Tell me what to expect at the border."

"They'll ask if someone has given you a package to bring into Canada. If so, they'll want to see it. You'll need proof of citizenship, such as a government ID or birth certificate. They'll ask about criminal convictions. If you've been convicted of a major offense you'll have to fill out an application and pay a fee. That'll delay entry. For some convictions, they won't let you in. Hunting and sport weapons can be brought in, but only if you intend to use them for that purpose while in Canada. You have to declare those weapons or they'll confiscate them and arrest you. Other weapons are illegal and you can't take them in."

"There won't be any problems."

"How can you say that? You're carrying the biggest knife in North America. Where are you going to hide it? They search every car. They know every hiding place. They even use mirrors to look under the car. I don't think you could hide it on your person. You could try taping it to your leg, but I think they'd get suspicious. I think they'd take you into a building for a body search."

"Leave it to me. I'm handling it."

"We can find a place to cross illegally."

"We'll cross ahead. I'm handling it."

"But what are you going to do?"

"I'm handling it."

Jim clamped his mouth shut. He shifted his gaze from the road to the land. The air was glossy. The plains were awash in the greens and golds of summer, too much for the eye to take in all at once. Jim's eyes went roaming, and he began taking things into his mind in pieces small enough to handle. Horse didn't seem real. Jim himself didn't seem real. The guy in Canada was made up. But the border station—that was real; it was in sight. Horse was calm; he looked as if he were engaged in a daily ritual. The knife was in his hands—twelve inches of blade, five of handle. He held it in a concise manner, awaiting his temptress with radical composure.

A ripple of awareness passed through Jim. He peered at the border station as if looking into a divining mirror. He glanced at Horse and saw a madman's never-ending dream of conquest and domination.

Jim removed his hand from his mouth.

"Horse, is it a being or a machine?"

Horse waved him off.

"Not now."

Jim rolled down his window as he pulled the Jeep to a stop. They were at the border station, and the world Jim knew seemed to dissolve.

As if in a dream, he watched four people rush out to greet him. In a flurry of activity, they untied the elk carcass, dropped it off the hood of the Jeep, and stepped back. A girl about nineteen with long dark hair and a slender figure told him thanks. Jim could not take his eyes off her. She was like a silk breeze from China. An old man kept shifting his gaze between the elk and Jim, appraising both. The girl's eyes began laughing. She said thanks again.

⧗

And that is when Jim hears the voice of a cop giving a warning. "Stay inside tonight. Someone's missing. Pets have gone missing, too. We think there's a mountain lion about."

And Jim is back in his cabin in the mountains of California and he is scrambling around the place searching for his notes on what is real.

"Is it a being or a machine?" he asks the cop, who has stepped inside the cabin, red and orange glows reflecting off his face.

"I don't know. Being, I'd guess."

"The invaders are beings," Jim says. He makes a note. "I think they're taking out the sentinels."

"That's what they're doing, all right."

"Laws have changed," Jim says. He eyes the cop. "We get in trouble now for doing no wrong."

"We always have. I have to leave now."

It is Spencer, Jim thinks. Not a cop, but Spencer, his older son. And Spencer reflected much back to him in the form of Horse. And Jim is glad Spencer did not kill him, but wishes Rory, his younger son, would come now.

He remembers words from Vinita. *A catastrophic event killed us all. We are all dead, and we are not used to being dead. That is why we are having tricks played on our minds.*

She did indeed play a magic trick on his mind; he knows that much is true. Is everything just a trick? Is nothing real?

He hears the closing of the door as the cop takes his leave. And then he hears a knock at the door.

Are we all dead? Jim wonders. Are the light beings coming to sweep us up with broomsticks quickly dancing?

Images form in his mind: The cabin door. The Jeep's door. Window time. Mirror time. The border station. The elk in his gunsights. Himself in Vinita's gunsights.

Everything's a door, he thinks. A doorway. To somewhere, to someone, to something. Death itself is a door. And he knows it's the only thing that's real. And he knows it goes on forever.

He rises to answer the knock at the door.

⧗

I hope you enjoyed my novella *Magical Elk*. If you did, please consider leaving a review on Amazon or on other platforms. It helps other readers discover it and supports my work as an author. Your feedback means the world to me!

Now please turn the page for an excerpt from my upcoming novel, *The Ribs of Man*.

Excerpt from

THE RIBS OF MAN

One

⧖ Pitch McKenzie ⧖

A Summer Evening in the United States

The doorbell chimed and woke Pitch McKenzie from his nightmarish thoughts. Who was it? Was it someone bringing news of treason in the nation's capital? Did conspirators and traitors in Congress cast their votes yet, outlawing private gun ownership in the United States of America, in total violation of the Second Amendment? Congress was meeting in secret session this very night to do just exactly that. The fix was in, the money spread around, dissent crushed through threats and intimidation.

Assassination teams and death squads were strategically placed around the country.

The fearful in Congress trembled.

The press was gagged; they trembled, also.

Pitch stood from his leather armchair in the living room and walked to the door. He flicked on the porch light, opened the door, and beheld a large man in a dark suit who held out a badge. Another large man in a dark suit stood lurking beyond the reach of the porch light.

"Sylvan Kring, Homeland Security," the man said, holding his badge close to Pitch's face.

Pitch read the badge, knew it was fake cover, but had no doubt that Sylvan Kring, or whatever the guy's name was, was a government agent. More than likely CIA. More than likely armed to the teeth.

"I'd like to see some ID," Kring said as he put his ID away.

Pitch said nothing.

A moment later, Kring said, "I have something to discuss with you. Can I come in?"

"No, you can't come in."

Kring turned to look at the man lurking beyond the reach of the porch light.

Something seemed to pass between them.

Kring turned to face Pitch again.

"All right, I won't screw around with you, Mr. McKenzie. We want you to become an anti-gun informant. Starting tonight."

"No," Pitch said.

"If you refuse, you will be considered an insurrectionist."

"I refuse."

"You'd better think about that, Mr. McKenzie. The government can freeze your bank accounts and credit cards, we can get you fired from your job, we can restrict your travel to essential trips for groceries and medical care only."

"Drivel."

"We can incarcerate you permanently without trial."

"Get out of here."

Kring turned to look at his partner again. Then faced Pitch.

"We will pursue the same course of action against your wife."

"What about my daughter?" Pitch said. "She's fourteen. Are you going to pursue the same course of action against her, too, you pathetic piece of shit? You pathetic excuse for a man. Get the fuck off my property."

Pitch closed the door, turned off the porch light, and heard Kring walk away. He threw all thoughts of Sylvan Kring from his mind and sat in the living room, his mind adrift.

Sometime later, a window across from him opened, the curtains set swaying.

Something entered.

He felt the coldest chill yet.

Yikes! He leaped to his feet, looked around, and shuddered.

His wife and daughter stood in the living room.

He thought they must have let themselves in through the front door.

No doubt they were here to try one last time to get him to give up his ridiculous conspiracy theories.

"Hi, Dad." Lacy spun through the room, looking for Pitch's guns. She'd been so afraid of them when he first brought them home six months ago.

"Hi, Lacy."

"Hi, Pitch," his wife, Savannah, said. "Are the guns gone?"

"No, Savannah, they aren't gone."

Lacy kept spinning through the room, looking for his guns.

"Pitch, they're weapons of war," Savannah said.

He watched his wife as she spun through the room, searching.

"Well, Savannah, we *are* at war."

He wondered if his wife had become a government informant, if she'd turn him in for having guns.

"Dad, you're an engineer, not a soldier," Lacy said. She had stopped spinning now, but kept turning her head, looking for his guns. "Let others do the fighting. You're not trained for combat."

Pitch was certain his daughter was not an informant. He could recruit her for the Resistance later, but he'd have to get her away from her mother.

"We're all soldiers now, Lacy. Our government and the globalist criminal cartel that controls it have declared war on us. It's going to get very bad, very soon."

Lacy approached him. "What will you do, Dad, when the shooting starts? I know what I would do. I would duck and hide. I would crawl away. You and I are alike. Heck, we're even afraid of the neighbor's dog, even when he walks up to us wagging its tail."

"We *are* alike, Lacy. We're not fooled by a wagging tail. Sinbad is a big, strong dog. He has a wagging tail. We're wary."

"You're going to get yourself killed, Pitch," Savannah said. "If you go out there tonight. If you go anywhere with those guns." Her voice was low keyed, calculated to make him give it up. She knew government killers would be out tonight. She knew they would shoot first, ask questions later.

"This is the hill to die on," Pitch said. "We are at war. The cattle cars, the death camps. They're real." He saw them clench their jaws. Neither believed him. They hadn't believed him six months ago, either, when he'd presented voluminous evidence.

Savannah blew her breath out audibly.

"You're not a soldier, Dad," Lacy repeated as she spun through the room again.

"We're all soldiers now, Lacy," he repeated. There wasn't much else to say.

Lacy puffed out her cheeks in imitation of her mother and exhaled mightily. She spun around again, still looking for his guns, and whispered, "What am I going to tell my friends?" Her undertone said, *My father is a kook.*

"Come on, Lacy." Savannah took her daughter by the shoulders. "We'd better go."

Pitch caught her tone. *He's dangerous. He's insane. We need to be protected from him.*

He wanted to shout at them. *Our government is going to slaughter us! They've got the death camps built! But I'm the dangerous one? I'm the insane one?*

At the door, they stopped and looked around again, their eyes conveying fear. Fear of those evil guns. The government-run psyop had been fabulously successful. The government knew the people better than the people knew themselves. They knew just exactly what buttons to push to evoke unreasoning fear.

"Wait," Pitch said. He took a step toward them. "Don't forget, if Ace Quillen should ever show up, you are to take defensive action. Ace is dangerous."

Ace Quillen was a CIA-planted spy at Pitch's engineering firm. When Pitch realized Ace was shadowing him, he warned his wife and daughter. Now he was warning them again.

"Bye, Pitch," Savannah said.

"Bye, Dad," Lacy said.

They left.

Pitch was alone again.

He remembered their parting words of two months ago.

When are we coming back, Mom?

When he comes to his senses.

His wife had clouded his name forever in his daughter's mind.

We are at war. Can't you see that? Hitler, Stalin, Mao, and countless other tyrants disarmed their populations first, then the slaughter began.

The U.S. Congress would start this grisly work in America tonight.

Tonight, they would pass a law in secret session that would ban all private gun ownership in America.

We are at war!

Pitch McKenzie knew he was unsuited for the dangerous task ahead. He wasn't brave. He wasn't a fighter. But he must become brave. He must become a fighter. His life depended upon it. Other lives depended upon it. He must transform himself into a man brave enough to fight the injustice that was going down tonight in the nation's capital. What happened tonight would change everything forever.

It was the hill to die on.

There was no going back after the sickening lies and deceits of tonight. What Congress did tonight would change the United States, and the entire world, forever.

The old Pitch must die.
The new Pitch must be born.
And it had to happen tonight.
That's all there was to it.

Two

⌛ TRICK EMERY ⌛

Trick Emery had been walking since before sunup and now it was near sundown. Fatigue had hit him long ago, but he pushed through it. Whenever he saw someone, he stopped and asked for a drink of water. Almost all were obliging, so long as Trick had something to trade.

Trick had maps of the local area, compasses that worked well, and 9mm rounds to trade. He had to keep his gun, though. He always told them that.

He could also teach skills, such as how to build a campfire, how to boil water over the campfire, how to gather edibles from the forest, how to build a lean-to, how to trap small animals, how to catch fish, how to gut and clean fish and game, how to find clean water from mountain streams, and so on.

He could even teach them how to brew beer, a skill that traced back thousands of years.

Trick heard sounds and swerved off the path. He saw a man and a woman stacking up dead branches under a big pot that was hanging from an iron tripod. He saw that the woman held an infant. Food, he thought.

He hailed the man.

The man hailed back.

"I'm in need of food," Trick said. "I can trade you a map, a compass, and 9mm rounds for food. I must keep my gun, though, and most of my rounds."

"We have food," the man said. "We'll have a fire soon. I can take 9mm rounds and a map and give you food. We have a compass. Come."

Trick walked up to them and told him his name was Trick Emery. He said he was traveling to Walk o' Giants.

The man stepped back a moment, possibly caught by surprise by what Trick had just said. Most people would not be so bold as to say they were traveling to Walk o' Giants. After another moment, the man said his name was Helmut Saint.

Helmut Saint said he was a Homeland Security agent. He said his wife's name was Maddie, and their infant son's name was Brian.

Helmut took another step away from Trick, a look of uncertainty darting from his eyes.

"Why did you tell me you were a Homeland Security agent?" Trick asked. Most people who dwelled in the Ribs of Man did not announce themselves by what they were on the surface world, especially if they were nefarious or notorious there.

"I don't know," the man said. He looked away.

"You're learning," Trick said. "Is your name really Helmut Saint?"

The man said yes.

Maddie set Brian down, gathered more branches for the fire. Soon, she had a blaze going and a pot of water boiling over it, then she was back tending Brian, tickling him and cooing to him. "Food soon," she said. She made as if to uncover a breast, looked up at Trick, smiled, and froze her hand in place.

The fire raged under the pot of boiling water.

Helmut was leaning over the pot of boiling water, stirring in vegetables.

Trick Emery walked up behind Helmut, pulled an iron rod from a sheath on his belt, and using both hands, swung it at the back of Helmut's head as hard as he could.

Helmut, maybe catching movement from out of the corner of his eye, ducked.

The rod clipped him. Helmut went down, gashed but not dead.

Maddie cried out, jumped to her feet, Brian in her arms. Brian erupted into wild squealing.

Trick ran at Maddie, who was screaming, frozen in place. He swung the iron rod at her head, heard the crack of her skull, saw her go down. She should have stayed down, but miraculously she began to rise slowly.

Helmut was rising slowly, also, blood trickling from his head wound.

Trick dropped his rod, pulled his knife, jumped at Helmut, rammed the knife into his ribs. He yanked it out, stuck him again aiming for the heart, held it in, twisted it.

Helmut moaned feebly and slumped to the ground.

He was dead or dying.

Trick went after Maddie, knifed her, twisted it. She slumped to the ground. Another dead or dying Saint.

Trick wiped the blood off his knife on a clean patch of Maddie's blouse, sheathed it. He jumped at Brian Saint, the infant son of Helmut and Maddie.

Brian squealed like a pig.

Trick carried Brian to the big pot of boiling water on the fire. He set the squealing infant into the water, and a while later pulled him out and took a bite out of him and dropped him back in. The infant bobbed around in the boiling water, squealing like a pig.

All this happened against the banging of a hammer on a blacksmith's anvil.

Trick looked around but saw no blacksmith.

Trick feasted on Brian and on the vegetables that Helmut had stirred into the pot of boiling water. He found fresh water to drink.

This was a good place to stay the night, he decided. He would sleep near the fire.

He looked around. The banging of a hammer on a blacksmith's anvil continued.

Trick sat and waited for either a blacksmith to appear, or for sleep to overtake him.

Three

⧗ PITCH MCKENZIE ⧗

Pitch sat in the living room, his mind aswirl with his darkest thoughts yet. An unknown number of extermination camps had been built in the U.S. More were being built every day.

Establishment sources said reports of extermination camps being built in the U.S. were conspiracy theories. Not true. That was disinformation being spread to not alarm the brainwashed masses. These camps were being built.

Pitch was a mechanical engineer and had visited several of these sites as a consultant. They told him the facilities were bioengineering research centers where new varieties of plant-based food would be created.

But Pitch's instincts told him to take a deeper look.

He pored over the plant layouts, the automated equipment, the material-handling systems, the chemical-handling systems. All told a story.

These facilities were death camps.

Other evidence supported this conclusion.

Pitch saw high government officials and elite scientists at these plants. What would they be doing at such stripped-down, foreboding facilities?

Clearly, the facilities were designed to process something in high volume. They had huge ovens, towering smokestacks, extensive receiving docks that opened onto rail lines, but no shipping docks.

These stark facilities were designed to receive something in by rail, but were not designed to ship anything out.

He reasoned it out.

The sites were isolated, away from big cities. They were surrounded by high metal fences topped by concertina razor wire. They had barracks and guard towers.

Could these sites be used for something else?

Like a good engineer, Pitch tested the idea.

What type of industrial plant processed commodities, such as wheat or livestock, using a process that required huge furnaces and smokestacks, but shipped nothing out? None that he could think of.

Another possibility gnawed at him. Could they be used for human experimentation, medical or otherwise, after which the human subjects would be killed, dissected and studied, and the remains incinerated and sent up the chimney? It was possible. But he could not get his mind around anything specific. The idea, horrific as it was, stuck in the back of his mind.

No. They had to be death camps. What else?

Could these facilities receive huge numbers of humans on

cattle cars? Could they gas these humans? Could they incinerate the bodies and send the ash and smoke up the smokestacks?

Yes, they could.

In his mind, he saw the evil design.

He thought it would take a hundred or so death camps to exterminate the American people in about one year's time.

They would be receiving humans in droves on cattle cars. After killing them, the bodies would go up in smoke. The sky would fill with ash.

It was an enormous undertaking. The extermination of over 300 million American men, women, and children, and the processing of their bodies.

Secretly, Pitch had begun tracking new construction of death camps, cattle cars, and rail lines all over America.

He gave warnings to close family and friends, and spread the word to prominent gun owners and advocates throughout America. Some of them said they already knew what was afoot.

Most of the American people were ignorant of the approaching danger. They'd been brainwashed by a relentless government psyop that vilified private gun ownership.

The government and corporate media had labeled gun owners insurrectionists. They said American gun owners were the single greatest threat to national security.

But the truth was something else.

The cattle cars had been built. The rail lines laid. The gas chambers readied. The ovens and smokestacks in place.

All that remained was to disarm Americans.

They think I'm the dangerous one, Pitch thought. But I didn't build the death infrastructure. The government did. And corporate America supported it. Once the death camps kicked into high gear, they'd restock America with compliant slaves from China and elsewhere, to keep the loosh farms going.

Loosh.

Pitch had heard the term bandied about at the facilities and had discreetly inquired about it. He learned it was the fear-based negative emotional energy produced by humans under duress, harvested by nonhuman parasites called Archons. It was the Archons' sustenance; they couldn't exist on this plane without it. It was said the Archons had always ruled the human race and had created all the wars, the famines, the disasters, and the entire scope of human suffering that maintained a steady supply of loosh.

Wild concepts such as loosh and Archons were too radical for Pitch to accept right off. But they did tend to resonate with what was going on.

After tonight, the government would enact emergency legislation giving them power to protect the people from insurgents.

For your protection, we will relocate you to camps, until we've dealt with the insurrectionists.

Millions of compliant Americans would be loaded onto cattle cars and taken to death camps to protect them from dangerous insurgents like Pitch, who'd never even owned a gun until he saw what was going on.

It was truly insane, but the American people—the sleepwalking masses—always fell for insane ideas, so long as they came from their own government, and they always lined up like sheep.

The compliant ones would be processed so quickly at the death camps they wouldn't even know what hit them.

Unwittingly, Pitch had helped the government design these

quick, efficient slaughterhouses. Initially, he did not know they would be used to slaughter the American people.

Now government killers would be hunting him down tonight to silence him.

Pitch wasn't the only one marked for death. CIA killers had staked out hundreds of the nation's most prominent gun owners and advocates. After killing them, they would seize their guns and ammo. The government would claim these people were killed during various insurrections.

Staged videos of gunfights between government agents and alleged insurrectionists had already been made and would be aired after the gun confiscation began.

Pitch's mind drifted away from extermination camps and wandered into a milky land of white bone and darkness. He shuddered. Dreams of white bone and darkness had been haunting him. He had them at night while he slept; he had them during the day, waking visions. They seemed to be premonitions. But of what?

He heard the tramping of feet outside the house, someone cutting through the yard. A chill shook him.

He went into the garage, got a broom, and brought it back to the living room. It was a yellow corn-straw broom with a long handle. He set it beside the front door.

He would take the broom with him when he left the house. It was a good defensive weapon to use against Sinbad, the neighbor's dog. Sinbad had tramped through the yard. The sound was unmistakable.

Sinbad was a good dog, but he was young and powerful and had the energy of a barbarian. The broom kept Sinbad at a distance. It gave Pitch more of a level playing field.

He had started carrying the broom around the yard to thwart a pesky squirrel that kept building a nest on a window ledge. He swept the nest away daily, and finally the squirrel gave up. But Sinbad moved in next door, and the broom acquired a new utility.

Pitch checked the time, went into the garage again, and brought back a rifle bag. Two AR-15 style semi-automatic rifles were inside, along with two 9mm pistols, spare magazines, and a lot of ammo.

These rifles and pistols, along with every other gun imaginable, were the weapons the U.S. government was going to make illegal for private citizens to own.

These rifles and pistols, and all other guns imaginable, were what private citizens would use to blow the heads off CIA killers and anyone else who came along threatening them with detention or death camps.

The Second Amendment to the U.S. Constitution gave the American people the right to keep and bear arms. Natural law also gave the people this right. Guns gave the people a fighting chance when their own government declared war on them.

Hitler had done that in Germany. He had declared war on the people. Stalin had done it in the USSR. Mao had done it in China. Countless other tyrants had done it to their people. Disarmed them, then killed them.

After tyrants confiscated the people's guns, the slaughter began. The death count was in the hundreds of millions.

And now history was repeating itself.

The globalist oligarchs that controlled the American government, the American media, and all other American institutions had done it. They had declared war on the American people.

Gun confiscation was underway. The death camps had been built. The unsuspecting American people would be led away for their protection, and slaughtered like lambs.

But not all Americans were oblivious to what was going on. A good portion of the population knew the truth and were ready to fight. But without guns, all was lost.

Even with guns, victory was not going to be easy. The CIA, FBI, and various other police agencies were armed with advanced military weapons and gear, including night-vision technology, drone support, and fully automatic weapons. These government killers, observed in the few skirmishes that had already happened, seemed more like robots than humans. They were relentless, merciless, indefatigable.

Guns must be kept in the hands of the people. Then there was a fighting chance. It was the hill to die on.

Pitch had vowed that he would become brave enough, tough enough, and decisive enough to fight this war all the way through to victory. Or he would die trying. He would call his fellow citizens to war. He would kill the enemy. He would sabotage their supply chains. He would spy on them, and he would plot their destruction. He would execute traitors within the Resistance.

For Pitch, the fight had already begun. He had already been spying on them. He had already been making plans.

Pitch made one more trip to the garage and brought back a full-sized humanlike figure with articulated limbs that he'd been keeping on a shelf by his workbench. The figure looked very much like Pitch. In the darkness, no one would be the wiser.

He'd made the figure a few months ago when his plan began to take shape.

He set the figure and the rifle bag near the front door and then sat down in the living room again, his mind returning to the death camps.

Early on, he knew the government had a problem to solve.

How could they control large numbers of people that were being led to their deaths? There would probably be hundreds, if not thousands, of people designated for the death chambers each time the cattle cars pulled up. At what point do sheep wake up and fight for their lives?

Machine-gunning them would do it, but that would be problematic. You'd have to drag the bodies away and clean up the mess, and then prepare to machine-gun the next group being unloaded from the cattle cars, after they'd heard the unmistakable sound of machine-gun fire.

You'd have a war on your hands then.

He figured the government must have done something to tilt the odds in their favor. What had they done to ensure that the sheep would stay asleep, that they would stay compliant from when they stepped off the cattle cars to when they stepped into the gas chambers? That in-between area was ripe for war.

Would plain, old-fashioned trickery be adequate to the task? Pitch doubted it. There must be something more to it. But what?

There always seemed to be an impenetrable wall of secrecy at these facilities, always something going on that he was not privy to. He began to finesse his way deeper into their culture to penetrate that wall. What he found was dark, hellish. It was like falling into an abyss.

It was that horrific idea again. Human experimentation.

Deciding to explore it, he thought he knew the most obvious place to start.

With the thespians.

While visiting the facilities, Pitch had mostly kept his silence, playing along so he could learn more. He had tuned in to the atmosphere of these places, and he had begun to notice subtle things.

What he noticed was very elusive. It wasn't normally seen unless you were looking for it. He encountered thespians in these facilities. Players in a game or a drama. People who seemed to act as if they were on stage, playing a role, reciting a script.

Managers, engineers, scientists, visiting dignitaries—any or all of them could all of a sudden jump out of character and become thespians.

It was so subtle. Elusive.

One of these thespians, a man named Willie Blackenship, seemed to play a central role in a drama that floated around several of the facilities. Willie Blackenship struck a robust figure, had a glowing complexion, blue eyes, and grayish-brown hair. Looking like a smirking wolf, he would sound off like a Nazi impresario, arranging speeches and rallies for *der Führer.* Joking, laughing, he'd say things like, "I use emotion for the many and reserve reason for the few." Pitch later learned this was a quote attributed to Adolf Hitler.

Willie Blackenship had made speech after speech at these facilities. At intervals, hypnotic music played during his speeches, a raised volume, then a lowered volume, then lowered below human threshold to subliminal levels.

Pitch knew he had heard these speeches of Blackenship's

before. He had heard the same tone and cadence anyway, in old newsreels of Nazis speaking to huge crowds in pre-World War II Germany.

Were they playing wargames at these facilities? Were the speeches a crucial part of the wargames?

Pitch, the engineer, put the idea to the test.

As an engineer, he had access to restricted areas, to documents, to important people who, conceivably, could talk on almost anything.

He became braver and began approaching the subtle, elusive thespians, including Willie Blackenship.

At several of these facilities, Pitch feigned support for the mass extermination of Americans, usually in a joking way. This caused elite scientists and government officials to open up to him and reveal plans, usually in a joking way, also.

They revealed mind-control techniques, trance inductions, giving orders in a certain way so people had to obey, such as strip naked, enter the showers.

He secretly recorded hours of what he considered wargaming at the facilities, audio and visual. From these recordings, he pieced it together.

His equipment had recorded protocols for killing Americans in the death camps. The protocols included inducing a trance. They included giving orders that subjects readily obeyed while in trance.

Pitch had seen the death protocols wargamed at the facilities, and from them, he had hatched a plot for use against government agents.

His plan was to use recorded special effects and his own voice to induce trance and give commands to the CIA killers who would be gunning for him. He believed almost all government agents would be under some kind of mind control.

Pitch thought government agents had been modified by either gene therapies that facilitated trance and obedience or by behavior-modification techniques. That was part of the globalists' multi-decade advanced planning for the end of America.

The Americans to be rounded up and transported to death camps would be altered for trance and obedience by a gene therapy or by behavior-modification techniques. The gene therapies could be spread by something innocuous, such as food, drink, or a spray mist. An entire herd of humans could be sprayed and altered in a matter of minutes.

Any subjects not yet altered when they reached the death camps would be altered unobtrusively when they arrived.

Pitch was certain that mind-control techniques, facilitated by gene therapies, were already being practiced at these facilities.

He thought the thespians, except for the top dogs, were probably mind-controlled slaves themselves.

Had Pitch himself been mind-controlled to obey? He didn't think so. Elite engineers using their creative intelligence to design the facilities' systems were probably left alone, but not completely. Also, if he was mind-controlled, would he be planning a resistance? Not likely.

He had learned something additional that might be useful when the time came to fight back. He had seen secret plans for gassing CIA death squads after they'd done their dirty work. He would tell them they were destined for the gas chambers, also.

The phone rang.

Pitch answered it.

"Hello."

"This is Zane. The bastards did it. They passed the law. The president says he'll sign it immediately. When he does, it's official. Then you and I and a hundred million other gun owners in America are legally bound to turn in our guns or they'll come looking for us. Don't you just love it? They know we won't turn in our guns. It's war. The killers are already coming. They plan to take us out tonight."

"I hear you," Pitch said. He waited to see if Zane had anything else to say.

Silence.

"We'll do it," Pitch said.

"Yeah, we'll do it."

They hung up.

Zane was a codename used by a government agent who was secretly a member of the Resistance.

Pitch and another engineer named Chris Llamas, who was also a member of the Resistance, would either kill or elude a team of government agents tonight and then head for New Mexico, where sophisticated elements of the Resistance maintained a hideout in the mountains.

Pitch picked up the phone and called Chris.

"Get here as soon as you can. The war in on."

Four

⧗ TRICK EMERY ⧗

Darkness dwelled in the Ribs of Man. The campfire dwindled. The pot no longer boiled. Trick Emery had consumed the infant Brian entirely, short of crunching up the bones and eating them. He'd picked the bones clean, though, and thrown them across the ground. The bodies of Brian's father and mother lay where they'd been felled by Trick's iron rod and knife. All the while, the unseen blacksmith banged on his anvil.

Trick awaited the appearance of the blacksmith. He wanted desperately to sleep, to renew his strength and energy, but knew he could not. He did not know the danger this blacksmith presented.

Time dragged on.

A portion of the sky filled with milky light. Within that milky light there shone a fiery red-and-white piece of iron being forged on an anvil by a blacksmith's hammer. The fiery display tracked across the night sky, descended, swept across the land, and settled near Trick.

Trick scrambled away, shielding his eyes with one hand, clutching his iron rod with the other.

A blue mist-shrouded vortex took shape around the fiery red-and-white piece of iron. It spun madly and opened up as if to show a glimpse of eternity, whereupon the vortex vanished, and a blacksmith, his anvil, and a good portion of a blacksmith shop, including a blazing forge, appeared before Trick.

The blacksmith stopped pounding on the fiery red-and-white piece of iron he held with tongs against the anvil, and looked at Trick.

Trick was in a fighting stance, holding his iron rod in one hand, his knife in the other.

"Who might you be?" Trick cried.

"Pete Corrigan," the blacksmith said. "Do you not recall me? I visited you a fortnight ago, Trick Emery. I forged the weapons you hold in your hands."

Trick looked at his iron rod, at his knife, and then back at the blacksmith. "I do not recall this. I must have been asleep."

"You were not asleep, Trick Emery. You were frightened by my appearance, and so your mind did not properly register what took place. But you accepted the weapons I forged for you as if they were your birthright, which in many ways they are."

Trick studied the blacksmith. Pete Corrigan was about thirty-five years old. He was tall and husky and had bull shoulders, powerful arms, and a craggy face. His gruff exterior seemed to hide something inside that was as warm as the fire in his forge.

Trick sheathed his iron rod and knife.

Pete set his hammer down, and with his metal tongs, set the fiery red-and-white iron he'd been pounding into the forge.

"What brings you?" Trick asked.

"I come with a warning. You must stay awake tonight. A man needs your help."

"A man here in the Ribs?"

"Yes."

"But how could a man ..."

"How could a man enter the Ribs of Man?"

"Yes."

"Do you not recall what the Ribs are about?"

"Hmmm ... It's been a long time."

"Yes, it's been a long time, hasn't it, Trick?"

"Remind me. What are the Ribs for?"

"Do you know what a shadow is?"

"Hmmm ... I know."

"We are shadows, you and I. We dwell in lands where shadows dwell. We sometimes dwell in the Ribs of Man, for that is a shadow land."

Pete Corrigan peered about.

"What have you done tonight, Trick?"

"I've killed tonight. I ate well tonight."

"I see. Yes, you are indeed the shadow this man needs."

"This man ... tell me more."

Look for *The Ribs of Man: A Novel*
by Jason Durant in 2026